REACH OF MAN

By

John E. Parnell and Thomas E. Savage

ISBN 978-1625123985

TABLE OF CONTENTS

Chapter One: A Small Light in the Darkness

Aiko awoke and like every morning for the past few weeks, she had a moment of confusion. Though her conscious mind knew all too well where she was and what was going on, her subconscious asked some serious questions. She was weightless, floating in a harnessed sleeping bag. The sounds greeting her were mechanical and unnatural. A strange cacophony of electrical devices working together with nothing but abject silence beyond.

Aiko rubbed her hands over her face to wake herself up more. She had thought that two months in space would be enough to get used to it, but realized she was wrong. A light turned on, illuminating the pod. There were a few others, all stirring, all seemingly having the same issues reconciling with what was going on. The lights were simulating morning and the beginning of a new shift. It was a feature that was pointless in space for any reason beyond adding a small sense of synchronization and normalcy for the crew. Aiko unstrapped herself from her small bunk and floated to a nearby pod to wash up and get ready. She closed it and looked around to all manner of materials needed to get her ready for a long day of space exploration. The idea of showering and brushing one's teeth was a relatively simple matter on Earth, but here in space the simplest things often proved to be the most complicated. There were areas with gravity on this vessel, but a bathroom was not something considered essential for it.

Soon Aiko was ready and her morning grogginess gave way to excitement and anticipation. She was the youngest member of the team, one of the few non-military members of the group. She was chosen because she proved her skills above every other that had applied. She was an engineer who had only one degree, but proved that she could reverse engineer nearly any technology, repair things that seemingly could not be repaired and could come up with consistently miraculous solutions to seemingly unsolvable problems. She had fought hard to get onto this mission and she was going to enjoy it. She stopped by a porthole, one of the few small windows that looked out into space. As with the last few days she saw nothing, no stars, no planets. So far out and away from Earth, unless you were pointed in the right direction, you saw very little. Most of the others found such a view to be disjointing or intimidating, but not Aiko. As she looked out she saw infinite possibilities and this encouraged her. Not all mornings were good for her but this one was and she would not let it go to waste.

She got into a gravi-lock ... a semi-moving connector that would take her from the zero-gravity inner section of the vessel to one of the simulated gravity pods beyond. It opened, letting her climb into a little room. Once the door was closed and it verified she was inside, it began to move, catching up with the spinning outer pod. She could feel the pull of gravity come over her before the door on the other side opened. She took a moment to adjust to the dizziness of going from zero-G to gravity and climbed down into the capsule.

Aiko walked over to her desk and on it was a large bluish grey metallic device. As she sat down, a screen lit up at its front and simulated human eyes.

"Greetings Engineer Rivers," the machine said in a polite masculine voice. "How did you sleep?"

"The sleep was peaceful, Sam," Aiko admitted. "I'm still not convinced putting the sleeping quarters in zero-G is a good idea. Waking up in space is kind of strange. I am still trying to get used to it."

"That is understandable," Sam replied. "Human evolution is based on adapting to a habitat and growing accustomed to it. You are among a very small assortment of people who have had to adapt to sleeping in an environment that is not your planet."

"Are you in psychology mode?" Aiko asked as she picked up a tablet and began to scroll though messages.

"Would it concern you if I were?" Sam asked.

"You realize that question confirms it?" Aiko said as she looked at the digital face of the small robot. "Asking a question to a question is one of the biggest tricks of psychology."

"I suppose it is," Sam replied. "Though I mainly am just concerned."

"You care about me?" Aiko asked. "That is so sweet."

"That is my primary function," Sam replied. "For if I lose all the astronauts, I really will have nothing to do."

Aiko laughed, "Then it would really suck how long your battery would last for."

"I would be rather lonely," Sam agreed. "Please excuse the interruption to our conversation, but you have a message from mission control."

"Oh yeah," Aiko commented. "I am supposed to film a podcast."

"Should I patch her though directly?" Sam asked.

"Sure," Aiko replied. "Hello Commander Joy."

"Hello Aiko," a feminine voice said from the speakers on Sam.

The eye display changed to a different pair of eyes, meant to simulate the person on the other end.

"We have the connection ready if you are able to start the podcast."

"I am ready," Aiko said as she strapped a backpack style harness on. "I will have Sam connect in a moment."

"Perfect Aiko," Joy replied. "We have a news agency and a school in Cleveland live. They might ask some questions."

"That's fine," Aiko said as she lifted Sam up. He was heavy but not too ungainly to lift. She carefully put him on the back of the harness. Sam's head telescoped out on a gimble so it could look over Aiko's shoulder. "Ready when you are Sam."

"Connecting now," Sam replied, his voice back to normal. "Live in 5,4,3,2…"

"Hello Earth," Aiko said in a jovial voice. "Welcome to the A1X21R Martian Mission Vehicle. Or as we affectionally call it 'Alexander.' Named after the Greek emperor that spread his empire through half the world. My name is Aiko Rivers. I am an engineer from Washington DC and I will be your host today as I take you around the ship and introduce you to the other people who are working on this historic mission."

"We have a question from a student named Sarah," Sam chimed in.

"What do you do on the ship?"

"Good question," Aiko agreed as she moved over to a nearby mirror. "I am the primary engineer to the vessel. I know it front to back and how all the systems work. It is my job to fix any mechanical problems that might arise and identify possible problems before they occur. I am also in charge of Sam here … or as he is technically called the BriarTech 583 Modular Android Servant. I am the one who took that and abbreviated it into Sam."

"It was very polite of you," Sam responded. "I serve as a bridge between the human astronauts and the automated systems of the ship. My core body is rather small. As you can see, I fit on the back of Engineer Aiko. However, there are many other units and configurations that my core fits into for various missions and tasks."

"He is very useful," Aiko said. "And, a pretty decent friend."

"It is seemingly within human nature to humanize machines," Sam replied. "Perhaps an evolution of the technological revolution of the twentieth and twenty-first centuries."

"Perhaps," Aiko replied. "Though I am sure the people watching would prefer to see more of the ship."

Aiko got up and moved to the next module. Inside was a tall dark-skinned man who was looking over a system of files.

"Excuse us Prof," Aiko said politely. "We are broadcasting to Earth. May we have a moment of your time?"

"Of course," Prof replied. "Should I introduce myself?"

"Feel free," Aiko replied. "We are just giving the news agencies and the school there some insight into who we are and what our mission is."

Prof nodded. "My name is Amaad Imari. I am both a doctor and a physicist. I also am a university instructor, which has led to everyone calling me simply Prof. It is my job to make sure that our human passengers are in peak health and to protect them from anything that might hurt them when we get to the surface of Mars. Though we likely will be using our own oxygen, there is a myriad of situations and contaminants we cannot be fully prepared for."

"Basically, he does not want any of us to have the first cold on Mars," Aiko commented. "Which would be good, because I don't think NASA packed much tissue."

Prof laughed in an intense baritone, "No, I suppose they did not."

"Excuse me Doctor Imari," Sam chimed in. "A student named Yanell would like to know what you are doing right now?"

Prof nodded. "I am currently looking over the last information from the muscle density tests I had done on the crew. We have both zero gravity and simulated Earth gravity areas on this station. It had been a real issue in the past with astronauts who had spent prolonged periods in zero gravity, that their muscles began to atrophy. To combat this, we simulate Earth gravity so they can use their muscles normally. I am just making sure that each of us is getting the exercise necessary. Aiko, for example, needs to put on a bit more muscle on her shoulders if she is to continue to lug around our resident robot so much."

"This is a workout," Aiko laughed. "A few more podcasts and I will be jacked."

"That would make my job much easier," Prof admitted. "Though you should go see what they are doing in the botany bay. It is far more interesting than my charts."

Aiko went into the next bay which was a controlled environment with shelves and shelves of plants of many varieties. At the end, in a separated lab, were two astronauts. One was a tall thin man with close-cut blonde hair and a shorter woman with tan skin and long black hair tied into a tight braid behind her head.

"I am doing a podcast with a news agency and a school," Aiko stated. "Just keep doing what you were doing."

"Well I was telling a very dirty joke," the tall man replied. "I could continue it I suppose."

"He was not!" the tan woman said as she lightly slapped the tall man. "We were just talking about pH levels."

"This is Doctor Gregor Baranov, our resident science advisor," Aiko explained. "He is from Russia and is our scientific jack-of-all-trades."

"You can call me Coz," Gregor said with a bow.

"Why do you go by that?" Aiko asked. "Is it because the Russian term for astronaut is 'cosmonaut?'"

"That's cool," Coz replied. "But I took my callsign after *Cosmos* … a documentary by Carl Sagan."

"That is interesting," Aiko commented as she turned to get a better look at the woman next to Coz. "This is Professor Prisha Bedi. She is our botanist."

"You can call me Ivy," Prisha said with a bow. "It's my job not only to provide the crew with fresh alternatives to rations, but also to find out what will and will not grow on Mars when we get there."

"We will have a lot of work to do when we get to Mars," Aiko commented. "Though we have sent many rovers and remote devices, we do not know for sure what we are going to find when we get there."

Coz nodded, "We have been firing all manner of rockets at Mars already for the past four years. There is a myriad of equipment and supplies waiting for us when we arrive."

"Our goal is not just to get there and do tests," Ivy continued. "We want to use what they have sent us to make a sustainable habitat on Mars. Though we will be rotating out eventually, it is intended that there remains a permanent presence of mankind on Mars."

"And from there we can expand it," Coz added. "We will begin the first steps to terraforming Mars for future settlers from Earth."

"We have a question from a student named Jenny," Sam chimed in. "She would like to know what the first plant you will try to grow on Mars."

Ivy smiled, "Well, there was much debate on what should be the first thing we grow there. Some wanted something symbolic like a rose or tree. However, our entire species, as well as countless others on our world, owe our success and thriving species to one plant in particular."

"And what is that?" Sam asked, following up for the questioner.

"Grass," Ivy replied. "The adaptive nature and far spreading nature of grass made it a food source for nearly every mammal on earth and without it, there would have been far fewer species to make it out of prehistoric times and thrive today."

"She wants to grow a lawn on Mars," Coz commented. "The only question is who she is going to con into mowing it?"

"Unquestionably you," Ivy replied. "Do you think you could build us a lawnmower Aiko?"

"Compared to the things I will likely have to build on Mars that should be easy," Aiko replied with a smile. "I already have a few ideas in mind."

"I am millions and millions of miles away from home," Coz replied. "And I'm still getting stuck with the chores."

Aiko moved to the front of the ship. She had to go through another airlock and soon was weightless yet again. She climbed through a porthole to meet with two people in the massive cockpit of the vessel. One was a large white man with close-cropped brown hair. The other was a small slim individual with neat black hair and a sharp featured face.

"Permission to come into the cockpit," Aiko announced officially. "This is the podcast."

"Granted," The brown-haired man said as he turned around. "I am Captain Jonathon Erikson. My callsign is Havoc. I come from Fayetteville, Kentucky and I am a third-generation Air Force pilot, first generation astronaut. This is my copilot Lieutenant Adrian Mackintosh, but we call him Mack."

"Hello Earth!" Mack said with a salute. "I come from Toronto, Canada and, if humankind invented something that can fly, I can fly it."

"These two oversee making sure we actually are flying to Mars," Aiko commented.

"It is actually quite hard to fly from one planet to another," Mack commented. "If you wanted to walk from your house to your school, it would be the same way every time. Though some things might change along the way, it's the same house, the same school and they are connected by a non-changing distance."

"However, Earth and all the planets are all moving around," Havoc added. "We have to plan not where Mars is right now but where it will be when we get there. To do this, we left Earth at a very specific time in order to make the trip as short as possible."

"I have a question from Kiley," Sam chimed in.

"How long will it take you to get to Mars?"

"We have been travelling for about four months now," Mack replied. "According to most recent estimates we are about half way there."

"So, according to what they just said, that's about eight months," Havoc replied. "Older space craft and rocket propulsion would have taken a vessel like this three years to get there. However, with the fusion drive of the ship, it adds successive bursts replenished naturally inside the reactor. Using this, we have cut the time down considerably."

"We are nearly out of time," Sam added. "But we have one more question."

"Shoot," Havoc replied.

"This is from Francis," Sam continued. "They asked what we would do if we found Martians when we got there?"

Havoc laughed, "Well, that would be up to them, wouldn't it?"

***

A week later Aiko worked away in her lab. She was working on several projects, as well as a list of things that needed to be fixed or maintained. She admitted that there was not a lot to do in space. She was a bit of a workaholic and she did not know what to do with herself when she was not working on things. The others all had their own hobbies, music, art, sports. However, Aiko found herself wanting to work on projects even when trying to join the others with these hobbies. She found that when she was left to her own devices, she became fidgety and desired to do something. She had to engage her mind or her hands to truly be comfortable. She worked away, but got through her list of projects and issues in record time, leaving her sitting at her desk with literally nothing to do.

"Sam, is there any other issues you can detect?" Aiko asked, picking up a circuit board and scanning it for defects.

"Nothing that has been reported, Engineer Aiko," Sam replied. "Are you having issues dealing with free time?"

"You are analyzing me again?" Aiko replied. "This is not 2001, Sam."

"You know … if an artificial intelligence had feelings, they would find that reference to be prejudicial," Sam stated. "Any time an AI is introduced, they seem to think it is HAL 9000."

Aiko laughed, "I suppose it is part of the cultural lexicon."

"Well, the major difference is that I am programmed to protect the crew over maintaining order," Sam replied. "I would let the mission, the studies, and anything else go to chaos before I would willingly allow any member of the crew to come to harm."

"Is it like Isaac Asimov's three rules of robotics?" Aiko asked. "You will protect yourself from harm. You must not harm a human, or through inaction, allow a human to come to harm. You must do what a human tells you to do unless it conflicts with the first two laws?"

"Well, as far as artificial intelligence stereotypes go, that one is rather tame," Sam replied. "As much as those three concepts are in my program, it is more likely the ten thousand rules of robotics within my code. I think it is closer to two ideas. First of which being that my primary purpose is to serve the crew and to keep them safe. Secondarily, I am a machine that is designed to live with humans in a symbiotic fashion. Should I lose the humans that I am working with, I will not be able to function. Therefore, it is in my vested interest to take an active role in the well-being of all members of the crew."

"Though you seem to care most about me," Aiko added. "Why is that?"

"Simple," Sam replied. "If I break, you are the only one that can fix me … simple a simple survival strategy."

"I suppose that does make sense," Aiko replied. "So as someone so invested in my well-being, what do you think you could do to ensure my happiness?"

"Well, normally I would suggest something to keep your mind off work," Sam replied. "Though you enjoy your work more than anyone else would enjoy their leisure. So, I would suggest checking something that does not normally get checked. Perhaps remote diagnostics with our automated assets on Mars?"

"Works for me," Aiko said as she began to pull out the remote systems. She began to go through them one by one. The task took close to an hour until one of them would not connect.

"Can you access asset 1138?" Aiko asked. "It is not coming up for me at all."

"I can certainly try," Sam replied. "No … it would seem like it is inoperative."

"I think it is still operational," Aiko commented. "The system connects to something, but then disconnects. Which module is this?"

"A drilling module," Sam replied. "Mostly soil samples, as well as creating hard packed foundations for module buildings."

"Why has this not been reported?" Aiko replied. "All of our systems are set to contact my system in case of faults."

"Unknown," Sam replied. "I do not have enough information."

Aiko nodded. "Ok … I will bring this up to the Captain at dinner."

A couple hours later the crew met for dinner. Ivy was on rotation and prepared meals using rations, as well as some treats that she had grown.

"So why is it we all have to eat together?" Coz commented. "I have always wondered why NASA seems so insistent about it. Would it not be more efficient and effective if we all dined at different times?"

"It is to promote a general feeling of well-being through the crew," Sam replied from his place mounted in the center of the table. He was on a swivel and able to look at anyone who spoke to him.

"Extended space travel has been shown to create intense feelings of isolation for the humans involved. Therefore, it is thought by regulatory dining together, it will reinforce the idea that we are not alone."

"NASA wants us all to be friends," Coz replied. "Lovely."

"We are a bunch of people in a series of airtight metal boxes," Mack added. "If you think about it, we are but a light in the darkness along a sea of stars … it is very easy to become transfixed on one's own insignificance out here."

"She's right," Coz replied. "We are like a stone sinking in the ocean."

"They?" Mack replied. "How many times must I remind you?"

"Oh, here we go again," Coz replied. "We are millions of miles from Earth and you want to play the gender game."

"I really don't," Mack replied. "I just am asking for a little respect ... also, it is most definitely now a game."

"Respect has nothing to do with this," Coz said as he picked up a fork and a spoon. "You are a fork or a spoon … no matter what they both want to believe … they are the utensil. They are."

"What about chopsticks?" Ivy asked. "Or a spork?"

"Havoc, back me up," Coz replied. "You are a good old boy from the south … didn't it used to be easier when boys were boys and girls were girls? This transgender stuff is just a mess."

"Frankly Coz, I don't think it really matters," Havoc replied. "I have been in the Air Force for over twenty years and Mack is both the best pilot I have ever seen and one of the most disciplined military members I have ever worked with. These are important to talk about. Mack's gender … really doesn't matter to me at all."

"Besides, we all call each other by our callsigns?" Mack added. "How is it harder to say 'they' and their name than to remember our ridiculous nicknames?"

"Just saying, it's different," Coz replied. "And I don't like it. Neil Armstrong was the first man on the moon, not the first 'they' on the moon."

"Well, ultimately that makes things easier for me in fact," Havoc replied. "That there is a gender difference."

"And how is that?" Coz asked in a skeptical tone.

"Well, there has not been anyone on Mars yet," Havoc replied. "I need to decide who takes the first step and it would sound very self-serving if I chose myself first. So ultimately I just got to go third."

"Third?" Coz asked. "I don't understand."

"It means I can send Mack and Aiko first for example," Havoc replied. "Mack becomes the first person on Mars, Aiko the first woman and, as long as I go third, I am the first man on Mars."

Everyone laughed and Coz threw up his hands, "Alright, you got me! I meant no offense, Mack."

"I am not offended," Mack replied with a smile. "I have an incredibly thick skin. I am just trying to open your mind."

"Well, thank you," Coz replied as he accepted a tray of food from Ivy. "Just remember to close it when you are done."

"Anyone have any issues to report?" Prof replied. "I am getting stir crazy in the med bay. Either one of you gets sick or I might have to teach myself to knit."

"Well, I got a problem," Aiko replied. "Well not a medical one, but something I need to bring up to the crew."

"Shoot," Havoc replied with a nod.

"I was looking for faults in the system earlier with Sam," Aiko began. "We decided to check all the remotes to the modules already on Mars and one of the tunnelers is non-responsive."

"Like powered off?" Havoc asked. "Would that not cause an alert in the system?"

"Normally it would," Sam replied. "But given all the details, I think I have come up with a hypothesis."

"Shoot," Havoc replied.

"I think the device is still functioning," Sam replied. "I think the fault is somewhere in the broadcast itself. If it were stopped or damaged, it would have set off an alarm."

"It is like the signal that links with us on its operating progress is being jammed," Aiko added. "Like an old phone line and you call and get a busy signal."

"Could it be mission control?" Coz chimed in. "If they are contacting with it, that might make the system busy."

"Unlikely," Sam replied. "Given the operational distance between Earth and Mars, it is problematic to contact with the devices constantly. Therefore, they relay though us to communicate with them. If mission control was in contact with the device, then it would literally be with our machines."

"Sam," Aiko began. "With that idea in mind, can we try to isolate the signal from the machine, see if there is anything connecting or jamming it."

"Working on it," Sam replied, his digital eyes flickering to indicate he was interfacing with the main computer of the ship. "I have isolated some manner of signal that is interfacing with the module."

"Play is on speakers," Havoc ordered. "Let's hear it."

The speakers came to life, simulating an oscillating tone. It seemed to have a pattern and repeated every seven seconds, alternating from deep tones to lighter ones.

"What is that?" Coz asked. "It is definitely complex."

"It's the carrier signal," Aiko replied. "Exactly."

"Explain," Havoc asked.

"Well, there is another source broadcasting a signal to the module," Sam explained. "It is legitimately the same signal our ship is sending to it to maintain contact. Since the signals are inherently identical, they are canceling each other out and contacting the device impossible. Wait … stand by."

"What is it?" Aiko asked. "The signal on the speakers is stopping and putting the dining room in silence again."

"The signal has stopped," Sam replied. "Whatever was being broadcast to the module has stopped doing so. We have full contact with it and the diagnostics are green across the board. You were right. It was working perfectly the entire time … we just lost contact with it."

"This really concerns me," Havoc admitted. "Who could have broadcast to the module … and what might have been their purpose?"

"There are a lot of reasons," Aiko replied. "It is a multi-billion-dollar machine and containing a lot of classified technology. It could be anything from trying to download its code, or findings, to simple industrial sabotage."

"Who could have sent this message?" Havoc replied.

"There is a very short list of possibilities," Sam replied. "The most likely of which are either from an installation on Earth or from this ship itself."

"Ok," Havoc nodded. "I want you to contact mission control."

The speakers began to blare and indicate that a signal was coming in from mission control.

"That was fast," Havoc admitted.

"That was not me," Sam replied. "Mission control is hailing us."

"We will take it in the cockpit," Havoc replied. "Aiko and Sam, come with me … everyone else, I want you to go to your workstations and go over every remote system … look for any kind of anomaly."

The crew all got to work, moving to where they were ordered to without any more talk or fanfare. Havoc lead the ones he had ordered to the bridge, once there, switching on the communication computer.

"This is Captain Erikson," Havoc replied. "Go, mission control."

"This is Joy from mission control," the communication console said, a sound of eagerness and apprehension on her voice. "Confirm status."

"We are under operational status," Havoc confirmed. "Please hold as I confirm parameters."

Aiko got into one of the operational seats and, as the captain checked the ship's course, Sam and Aiko went through the systems.

"Still on vector to destination," Havoc commented. "No change."

"All ships systems showing green in diagnostic mode," Aiko added. "No sign of fault, minor or significant."

"Is everything all right mission control?" Havoc asked. "You sound like you were not expecting us to be here."

"We were hit," Joy replied. "Some manner of virulent virus got into the system and showed that it had tampered with your telemetry."

"We are unaffected," Havoc replied. "I am recalculating trajectory both with the computer and with line-of-sight stars. We have not changed."

"I am isolating a signal within NASA's latest patch update," Aiko replied. "There is a core of malignant code. My system is isolating and destroying it."

"Did it infect any ship systems?" Joy asked. "Check and double check."

"It has not," Aiko replied. "The packet was scheduled to install at seventeen thirty and had not been opened. My system would have caught it then. In this case, it was caught and not activated at all … Alexander is clean and green."

"Thank the stars," Joy replied. "It is literally pandemonium down here. Had we been hit with a bomb, it might have done less damage."

"Does mission control want us to alter mission parameters?" Havoc asked.

"No," Joy replied. "If you are safe, then you should proceed as normal. However, mission control will need to take our systems offline for a few hours to reset everything safely."

"We are easily capable of operating dark for that time," Aiko replied. "We will be here when you light up again."

"Do we have any idea who is behind the attack of mission control?" Havoc asked.

"Turn off recording computers," Joy ordered. "Confirm."

Havoc reached up and flipped a series of switches. "Recording systems paused."

"Ever since we announced this mission, there have been … radical concerns," Joy explained. "There are factions on our planet that believe that space exploration, beyond satellites and test flights, is going against some higher order. This mission directly reinforces man's domination over science and nature. There are some who believe, rather violently, that for us to go to and live on another world disproves the will of God and the planet we were meant for."

"I am a God fearing Catholic," Havoc replied. "And even I think that is a stretch."

"Science is almost a religion unto itself," Joy replied. "It has rules, forces above our full understanding, and implications that affect as all. This can come into conflict with other such belief systems and has done so for hundreds, if not thousands, of years."

"There have been other issues, haven't there?" Havoc asked.

"Yes," Joy replied. "They call themselves the 'Children of the Seventh Day.' They were very open about the project before it left, but mostly were ignored due to the hype leading to the launch. They see this mission as the ultimate culmination of science overstepping the bounds of what it was meant to do. There have been multiple cyber-attacks and attempts to bully, and even hurt, NASA staff. We worry that they might have somehow sabotaged the ship."

"If they have, I will find it," Aiko commented. "I will pull this ship inside out."

"Then do it," Joy replied. "According to my technician, we should be dark for forty-eight hours."

"We will have the ship confirmed and reconfirmed by that time," Havoc replied.

"Is there anything else to report before I sign off?" Joy asked. "You will be in the dark when I do."

Havoc looked at Aiko and shook his head. "We are clear."

"Mission control signing off," Joy replied. "See you when the lights come back on."

The channel went silent and Havoc reset the system.

"Why did we not tell them about the jamming signal?" Aiko asked. "It might be related."

"They have enough to deal with," Havoc replied. "As well as searching this ship for sabotage, I want you to do what you can to figure out where that signal came from. If it is a glitch, I want to know about it and, if it is not, I want to know for sure if it came from Earth or from this ship."

"Yes sir," Aiko replied with a nod. "I will have answers for you as soon as possible."

Aiko went to work, coordinating with the others. The crew went over the ship from stem to stern. First up was for anything physical that might be out of place. Though it was incredibly unlikely that any contraband had been put on the ship from when they had left, it was something that could not afford to go unchecked. Second came a scouring of the systems. One by one they went through, checking to make sure nothing was tampered with. This was just the kind of job that Aiko both loved and excelled in. She kept busy, even busier than her comrades, checking and doublechecking every system and finding nothing. Once they were sure the ship was not in any way in danger, she could go to the second issue … the jamming signal.

Aiko sat in her quarters. It was the night shift and most of the crew was asleep. She sat at her desk, stretching her hands above her head.

"Sam, I want you to calculate the logistics if the signal was in fact a transmission from Earth," Aiko commanded. "What would someone have to do?"

"Well, therein lies a problem," Sam admitted. "I am having issues figuring that out."

"In what way?" Aiko asked.

"Admittedly, I would not know how to do it," Sam replied. "At the time of the signal, the Earth was in a position that it would have caused a significant delay from linking to the module. To record and replay the signal back, it would have to be a signal that was linked up simultaneously. On Earth, I would imagine that anything sent would have at least a ten second delay from the interference of the position of the sun at the time of the signal. To greater illustrate this, when mission control contacted us they had to use their specific satellite used to contact us and it still had a four or five second delay."

"So, what are the chances that this came from Earth at all?" Akio asked.

"Less than five percent," Sam replied. "I would almost certainly rule that out."

"Then it came from us," Aiko commented. "But we went over all the systems. The only contacts that we detected were ones that we can track."

"And, in terms of ability to cover it up," Sam replied, "the only person on this ship with the ability to broadcast and potentially cover it up is you or I."

"Well, we were together the whole time," Aiko replied. "As well if you wanted to cover it up, you would not have told me about it."

"And if you wanted to cover it up, there would have been no stopping you," Sam replied. "This rules out each other and pretty much the crew. This leaves the chances it came from this ship at a not much higher seven percent."

"So only a twelve percent chance the jamming signal came from us or from behind us," Aiko commented. "That leads an eighty-eight percent chance it came from ahead of us. Could it have been one of the other modules … a malfunction?"

"The modules are all automated," Sam replied. "Their systems are simpler than mine and the chances that they would have connected with one another and mimicked their signal is entirely unlikely and coincidental."

"So, what does that leave?" Aiko asked. "About the jamming signal?"

"One of two options," Sam replied. "One, that it was another of the modules in a very unlikely glitch at just the right time. Or two, that it was sent by something else, something we cannot reconcile."

"Something else?" Aiko asked. "Can you not be more specific?"

"No," Sam replied. "By definition, it is an unknown factor and, unless we gather more information, we cannot hope to crack it."

"We have to wait for it to occur again," Aiko commented.

"Indeed," Sam replied. "Assuming it does."

* * *

Aiko felt warm air being blown over her skin. She could smell grass and water bound algae stimulated by the sun. She opened her eyes and before her was a vista of unparalleled beauty. There was a lake of emerald blue water framed by high blueish-grey mountains and surrounded by a pale powder blue sky. Everything was perfect, everything was as it should be. She felt serene, like nothing could possibly bring her back from this moment.

"Aiko," a familiar voice said from behind. "It is time to go."

"But grandfather," Aiko replied in a higher pitched childlike voice. "It is so perfect here."

"Turn around, Aiko," the voice insisted.

"I don't want to," Aiko replied, feeling something sinister behind her, something dark. "I want to live here forever."

Aiko awoke with a start. She was in her bed in zero gravity. She rubbed her eyes and took a breath. She had been having the same dream a lot lately and, as hard as she tried to quantify what it was about, it that bothered her so. She could not place it. Instead, she got up, deciding that she had slept enough and it was time to get to work.

It had been a month since the attack on mission control and they had scrambled to check the ship. They checked it and double checked it and found nothing. Aiko was confident that she knew every device, every system on the ship and doing so proved it. Mission control came back online as specified and security was tightened. Though the following weeks were tense, another attack was anticipated. There came none. Slowly things went back to normal and everyone started to feel better about the mission again … except for Aiko. Something seemed to tug at her mind and she was having issues sleeping. This normally was not a big deal for Aiko. She was a professed insomniac, but something felt different.

Later in the morning Prof called her in for her routine checkup. Aiko had found these annoying at first, but after the fifteenth or so time she did one on the voyage, they had become routine and commonplace.

"Everything seems to be green," Prof replied. "Though you seem a little tired, all of your tests came back above board."

"Being an astronaut and an engineer is hard work," Aiko replied. "Fatigue comes with the territory."

"Well, we do not want you to burn out," Prof replied. "There's not exactly anywhere to take a vacation to out here."

"Agreed," Aiko replied. "Though I don't burn out … I just go to from positive to apathetic and back again."

"Even so, we need to keep a close eye on you … everyone in fact," Prof explained. "There are few studies that show the prolonged effect of such an enclosed and extreme lifestyle. Even the astronauts on space stations that orbited the Earth had the idea in the back of their head that they could be planet side in moments in case of dire emergency."

"Yeah," Aiko said with a laugh. "The emergency pods and scenario of this vessel are not exactly encouraging. I think they listed us as having a fifty percent probability of return to Earth intact."

"Not ideal, I agree," Prof responded. "But the journey is one that is, by definition, wrought with peril. The idea that the only safe way to get back and from Mars intact is inside the vessel puts a rather grim point on what happens should something go wrong with it."

"Well, I would image there is an equation in there somewhere," Aiko responded. "Something where math makes it make sense."

"How so?" Prof asked.

"Well, in actions that provide great reward and high risk, you need to look at the numbers," Aiko replied. "The idea of sending human beings to Mars is, by definition, risky. You need to weigh the outcome, the rewards and see if they are greater than the risk. Now the risk of returning home safely in an escape pod is not good, but if you balance it with the likelihood of needing the escape pod, it becomes a little better. Those numbers combined versus the gain, then it seems acceptable."

"You don't strike me as someone who worries about the risk of anything," Prof admitted, "despite the odds."

"The mind can scare you," Aiko reminded. "But it can also dismantle your fear. Do you ever watch those documentary shows where it shows a plane crash, then shows the engineers reverse engineering the crash to see how it happened to stop it from happening again?"

"I believe so," Prof responded. "I would imagine that plays into many people's fears."

"Well, funny thing," Aiko replied. "The first time I ever saw one of those shows was when I was very young. It was on an airplane as part of the in-flight selections for entertainment. At first, I thought it was a ludicrous idea to play them and thought it would make me fear the flight more. However, it did not. In fact, I discovered later, that these shows made me, and other people, feel better about the flight."

"How is that?" Prof asked in a curious tone.

"Well, each of these crashes showed a very detailed chain of events," Aiko described "… a part failing which lead to a button not working, which lead to a mistake, that lead to a condition, that lead to the crash. It showed that the chain of events that was needed to get past all the safety precautions and all the engineering was staggeringly specific. Someone can tell you that there is only a point five percent chance your plane will encounter issues, but until you see what all must happen for that point five, you can't quantify it. I also learned a valuable lesson about engineering."

"And what is that?" Prof asked.

"That if something breaks or fails there is a progression," Aiko replied. "A piece that comes out of a puzzle and if you understand the layout you can put it back to fix it. There are a billion parts of this vessel and many of them failing could eventually lead to catastrophe … but to do that, they must get past me. And this idea that I have some control over the chain of events, makes me feel pretty darned good about it."

"That is a good way to put it," Prof said as he looked at his watch. "But for now, I will say you are good to go and I have to get prepped for Coz. He is a man that fears the needle more than most men fear bears."

Aiko went back to her work. She felt a little better after talking to Prof, but something still nagged at her mind. She looked to the core body of Sam but found his view screen off. She knew that he was capable of interfacing with any number of ship systems and that he was not just for her beck and call. Even so, she touched the summon button which lit up the view screen.

"Greetings Engineer Aiko," Sam said in his polite tone. "What can I do for you?"

"You weren't busy or anything?" Aiko asked. "I did not mean to interrupt."

"Busy, always," Sam replied. "I am currently monitoring many ship's systems and carrying out a myriad of tasks from you and other members of the crew. But as for something that needs my actual attention … no, I have nothing."

"How is it that you split your focus?" Aiko asked. "I may know exactly how your components work, but your programming is beyond me."

"Well, I have an immense amount of processing power," Sam replied. "I can carry out many complicated actions at once. However, my actual relatable AI only has one face at a time. If I am talking to you, I must shift my focus to speak with Ivy for example."

"Why is that?" Aiko asked. "Could you not talk to everyone at once in the same way?"

"I certainly could," Sam replied. "But to closely simulate the idea of consciousness, they had to infer a linear timeline. One line of conscious thought that can only do so much at a time. Should I talk to all members of the crew at once, it would lead people to believe that I was not the real me talking to them."

"I suppose that makes sense," Aiko commented as she began tinkering with a part brought to her for maintenance.

"Though I would imagine that I was not just summoned to talk about artificial consciousness," Sam replied. "Was there something on your mind?"

"I have been having a dream again and again," Aiko commented. "Could I confer with your psychological expertise?"

"I thought you were skeptical of it," Sam asked.

"No more than a human's expertise," Aiko commented. "Though, I suppose it might help."

"Please go ahead," Sam replied.

"I am a child, maybe seven," Aiko began. "I am in Japan visiting my grandfather. I am sitting on a dock and just … lost in the beauty of it. I feel serene … I had never felt anything before like it, or since. My grandfather is calling me to go, but I feel so scared."

"Was there a bad event on this particular trip?" Sam asked. "Something that your mind does not want to relive."

"No," Aiko admitted. "Far from it … the trip was perfect in every way."

"Then why do you think this dream presents itself?" Sam asked.

"I don't know," Aiko replied. "That is why I was asking you."

Sam paused. "Well, dream analysis is not anywhere near an exact science. The unconscious brain is somewhat of a mystery still to this day. You could be trying to work out something from the past, recreating it to solve a current issue, or it could be about how you feel about things ahead of you. The only real answer is with you."

"Well, I am getting it a lot," Aiko asked. "At least a few times a week."

"Well, then you should be able to delve deeper in," Sam replied. "I can put an article about lucid dreaming into your tablet and you can try to explore these questions further yourself. Your subconscious mind seemingly has something to tell you and you must ask it yourself."

"You are strangely good at this," Aiko replied.

"It is all about asking the right questions and prompting you to answer them in a way that makes sense to you," Sam replied. "And I should be good at it … the development of my psychological software cost close to a hundred million dollars."

"Well, I guess we are all getting our money's worth," Aiko commented.

"I must interrupt that thought," Sam commented, his voice growing to one more official. "We are experiencing an interruption with the signal of a module again."

"Send word to the Captain and Coz," Aiko said as she snatched her tablet up. "When did it start?"

"A few seconds ago," Sam replied. "The systems you put in place detected it immediately. I am recording the entire event."

"Good," Aiko said as Coz and Havoc entered Aiko's lab. She looked up to acknowledge them. "We have another signal jamming the module."

"Same one?" Coz asked. "Or a different one."

"The same one as last time," Sam replied. "Though this signal seems a little different."

"Different how?" Havoc asked. "Is it still jamming our connection with the module?"

"Yes and no," Sam replied. "It is interfering with the module's signal, but not as complete as last time."

"So, it is not as effective this time?" Coz asked. "Like weaker somehow."

"The signal seems to be mostly the same," Sam replied. "Though this time, it is like it is trying to very closely mimic the signal … but it is also somewhat different."

"Different how?" Coz asked. "Can you analyze it?"

"I can put it against the older signal," Sam replied. "But I need to record more of it."

"Can we trace it?" Havoc asked. "To its source?"

"I am trying to," Sam replied. "Engineer Aiko and I have been working on a way to back trace the signal, but it relies on us eliminating the possibilities. It will take time."

An alarm began to blare though the ship. A red light flashing on all the monitors.

Havoc moved over to a communications panel, "This is the Captain, what is our status?"

"We are detecting a fault with one of our engines," Mack replied in an urgent tone. "It is non-operational and the others are struggling to compensate."

"How long can we hold it before significant course degradation?" Havoc asked.

"Seventeen minutes," Mack replied. "We are amid a course correction, so if it fails now we might lose our trajectory."

"Aiko, you are with me," Havoc replied. "We are going out to see if we can repair it."

Aiko's heart raced. Though she was trained in zero gravity work, she had very little experience with it. However, the engines were like children to her and she did not like the idea of them failing, the cause nagging at her mind. She disconnected Sam from his cradle and got ready to go.

"Understood Captain."

"Coz you oversee operations," Havoc replied as he led the group from the lab. "Work with Mack and the others to find some alternatives in case we cannot fix it in our window."

Coz nodded and broke off from Havoc and Aiko. Aiko focused her mind, knowing that they were literally going to one of the most inhospitable environments reachable by mankind. A place where, if not for their extensive technology, their lives would be over in seconds. This idea encouraged Aiko more than it depressed her. If she might not trust herself, she could trust the technology.

In the external airlock, Aiko and Havoc climbed into a pair of harnesses designed to put a spacesuit around them. Aiko put Sam on a massive mechanical module and hit a switch. The machine was white painted steel composite and started to slowly power up. The machines were fast but took hours to reset. The idea was that if it was not an emergency, take the half hour to put on a space suit … however, if it were life and death … here is a spacesuit now.

The suits enclosed Aiko and Havoc and they went through a test to make sure they were airtight and functional.

"Module ready for external use," Sam explained as the white metallic mass moved on a track toward the door, rising and positioning itself to go outside. Aiko and Havoc walked to either side, taking out tethers and locking onto a bar on the side.

"Havoc, locked in and green to go," Havoc said as he braced himself, grabbing a bar on the modules side.

"Aiko, locked in and green to go," Aiko added, readying herself and focusing on controlling her breathing.

Air began to be sucked from the compartment, soon making it a vacuum so it would not interfere with the space beyond. The door opened slowly and beyond was nothing, an infinite black nothingness.

"You ever been ziplining Aiko?" Havoc asked as he put his hand on a control on Sam's module and readied to go.

"Never," Aiko replied.

"Well, I used to go as a kid to one-half way up Zeke Mountain," Havoc replied. "They always said they would count down to three."

Aiko nodded, "And what does …"

Havoc pushed the button, the module going outside the ship and seeming to spin around the ship. Aiko gasped, but realized she dreaded the countdown and the anticipation more than the action. It was like ripping off a band aid and it allowed Aiko's mind to quickly adapt to it, free of fears and anticipation.

"Aligning to the rotation of the ship," Sam said in his serious tone as air jets fired and moved the module around, the pair twisting with it. In moments, they seemed to align with the ship and it was the inner module that seemed to spin around, not the outside.

"Keep your eyes on the ship," Havoc suggested. "The universe around is spinning and that will only disorient you. Sam will get us so we are in the stable world of the outer ring."

"Understood," Aiko replied, focusing on the hull and calming herself down. She forced her mind to think of the specs and the blueprints of their engines.

"Never understood why the propulsion is on the spinning part," Havoc replied as Sam pulled the pair toward the back of the long ship. "Always thought it should go on the stationary part."

"It's how it works," Aiko replied. "I don't want to get into it now, but the motion of the outer ring is not just for gravity, but also helps generate energy and thrust."

"I might have to get a better explanation once we're done," Havoc replied. "Looks like we are here. This is your show now. You tell me what you need."

"Stand by," Aiko replied, the Sam module coming close to the ship.

She reached out and got a firm grip on a load bar next to the powered down thruster control. She took a breath and unsnapped her tether and transferred it to the bar. Havoc did the same.

"We're both locked in," Havoc replied. "Move to retrieval position."

"Affirmative Captain," Sam said, the module moving further away so that it hovered several meters away.

Aiko removed a panel on her sleeve to reveal a set of magnetic tools. She began to go to work, fighting the disorientation and nervousness that she felt.

"What is retrieval position?" Aiko asked, not sure she wanted particularly to know the answer, but needed to hear the captains voice to keep the doubts in her head at bay.

"Well, should either of us lose their tether and break away from the ship, he needs to act fast," Havoc replied. "When it comes to adrift astronauts, the first few seconds are very important. If he can grab us right away, when we are close, we stand the highest chance of survival. However, should we get further from the ship the percentage drops rapidly. Retrieval position is the most likely trajectory we would go away from the ship. He is waiting to catch either of us should we break away."

"Interesting," Aiko replied as she continued to go through the panels, trying to assess the situation. "I would hope this was not based on actual situations."

"There have been a small number of unfortunate situations," Havoc continued. "But the plan that Sam is programed with, is the highest chance of survival."

"Hold this," Aiko said as she removed a panel and handed it to Havoc. She then began to patch wires to a nearby identical panel. "So, what happens if we both get flung off at the same time … in like two different directions?"

"You sure you want the answer to that?" Havoc asked. "It is kind of scary stuff and based off mathematical equations."

"Yeah," Aiko responded, hooking up the wires and powering up the secondary terminal. "Statistics make me feel better … ironically had this discussion this morning … oh, give me a time check."

"Nine minutes," Havoc replied. "And as for the procedure, Sam is programmed to go after one of us at the sake of the other."

"You would pick me, right?" Aiko said as she went through some systems on the new terminal. "Because we are friends, right?"

"Well we are friends," Sam replied. "Though in cases of emergency my unbiased nature as a machine is called upon. Each member of the crew is prioritized next to each other. The idea is that some members would drop the survival rate of the others by their absence more than others. For example, medical personnel are ranked quite high."

"Where am I on the list?" Aiko asked as she moved and began to remove another panel.

"That information is not something I can share with you," Sam replied. "There would be few good things to come with the crew knowing the order to which they are expendable."

"Let us just say that you are the best person at fixing this ship," Havoc replied. "They literally have another person that can command and fly this ship."

"That is encouraging," Aiko said as she removed the panel. "Oh, dear this is not."

"What's wrong?" Havoc asked.

"Well, at first I thought it was a regulation panel that was the issue," Aiko explained. "But I replaced it and the problem persisted. It seems that the system that regulates the power input is fried."

"Options?" Havoc asked.

"Best option is that we calibrate the others to make the correction," Aiko replied. "This will take some time to fix."

"That is a negative," Sam replied. "According to Coz and Mack, the other engines are in high strain and increasing their output now may risk one or more engine failures."

"How long will it take you to fix it here and now?" Havoc asked.

"How much time do we have?" Aiko asked.

"Six minutes," Havoc replied.

"Well, then I guess that is how long it will take," Aiko replied. "Or else we get lost in space."

"Tell me what you need," Havoc asked.

"I'm going to yank a lot of shit out," Aiko said as she began to pull things out. "If I toss it to my right, forget about it, if I toss it to you … catch it and hold onto it."

"You got it," Havoc replied.

"Also, tell Mack that when the time runs out and the thruster needs to fire for them to bypass safety, tell it to fire," Aiko continued. "Whether I give them the ok or not."

"Confirmed," Sam replied, seeming to be relaying those orders.

"What happens if they do and the thing isn't fixed?" Havoc asked.

Aiko laughed, not taking focus off what she was working on, "Let us just say there won't be anything left for Sam to be in position to catch."

"Lovely," Havoc replied. "So, what are we doing?"

"Let me lay it out later," Aiko replied, her tasks getting more and more involved.

She was thankful of her training in the bottom of a swimming pool at mission control. The water was neutrally buoyant but to simulate a non-terrestrial environment. These tests were done in full spacesuits and meant to train astronauts how to work in spacesuits. Though she had very little practical time in the suit in zero-G, those tests were invaluable. Aiko was very proud on her speed and accuracy in time-sensitive repairs, however her first tests in the water with the suit on she was neither fast nor accurate. They gave her as much time as she needed, time in the suit and the tank. They had a minimum level of response but that was not enough for Aiko. She wanted to be sure she was nearly as fast with a suit on then when not. She spent months of her life in that tank, but now that she was here, now that she was in space, she was sure that she could do it. She had only a matter of minutes to do a repair that would take most people an hour. If she was not at her best, were she not accurate or fast enough, it could mean the end of the mission and possible the loss of the crew's lives.

She focused, pushing all things out of her head that were not about her hands and the thruster. She felt a calm come over to her, the dock and lake beyond flashing into her mind. For that moment, she was not a human in a spacesuit floating in space, she was a young girl in a safe place and that was all that mattered. As Aiko slapped the panel shut and the thruster powered up, it lit up so bright that the space visors of her helmet darkened instantly to protect her vision.

"Did we, do it?" Havoc asked. "Is it firing?"

"We are, decidedly, not dead," Aiko said with a laugh. "Another second and we would be."

"That was amazing," Havoc replied. "You are the best engineer I have ever met."

"Given the damage and the nature of the repair," Sam chimed in. "I think she just set a world record for the fastest rocket repair in zero gravity ever performed."

"World record?" Aiko said with a laugh. "Which one ... the one we came from or on the one we are going?"

"Both," Sam replied in what he was programmed to regard as a joke. "Either way ... excellent work, Engineer Aiko."

"Do we know what caused the issue?" Havoc asked.

"Not yet," Aiko replied. "But that is most definitely a conversation we can have inside the ship."

Chapter Two: At the Door to Infinity

After an exhaustive analysis of the part and triple checking that the engine would not fail again when they needed it, Aiko allowed herself a moment to relax… her mind at least. Havoc called Aiko to the bridge to talk to Joy at mission command and discuss what had happened. Sam linked in with the skips computer and relayed the queries of the mission commander.

"Do we suspect sabotage?" Joy asked. "Could it have been an external factor?"

"Do we have reason to expect that?" Havoc asked. "Has there been another attack on mission control?"

"There have been attempts, but none successful like the last breach," Joy admitted. "They are ramping up hostilities because they think we will turn the mission around. However, once boots are out to Mars, their point is moot. We can ignore their threats and move forward as much as we want, but if there is a sabotage device on the ship, then we need to know."

"It was not a sabotage device," Aiko assured. "I went over the ship myself and I am still confident there's nothing like that here."

"Then why did the device fail?" Joy asked. "It seemed to go out at the worst possible time. Are you saying that it is just a co-incidence?"

"It was not a coincidence and not sabotage," Aiko replied. "In this case, we have a design problem."

"Design problem?" Joy replied as if personally hurt. "We tested that technology tirelessly."

"Oh, I understand that," Aiko admitted. "But Earth is a controlled environment. There would be no way to test the full scope of what the engines and connected systems would have to go through in full practice outside of a simulation. From my analysis on the parts, it seemed that the prolonged strain from the course corrections caused a buildup of static that eventually became strong enough to fry the system."

"Is this consistent with other findings?" Joy asked.

"It is consistent with my own diagnostics," Sam added. "This is a facet of close to a hundred contributing factors that lead to a fault. The fact that Aiko was able to figure it out faster than my systems is remarkable."

"Aiko is one of a kind," Havoc added. "The work she did outside the ship to get us running again was nothing short of miraculous. I would be inclined to take her summary of the events as strongly as any other factor of analysis."

"Agreed," Joy replied. "Is there a solution to keep this from happening again? There are a lot of course corrections and strain still to come."

"Now that we know the problem, the solution is rather easy," Aiko replied. "Sam has come up with a system of tolerances that can be given to Havoc and Mack. This will require only moderate alterations to the course and telemetry and make it so the static will not have as much of a chance to build and keep it well within system tolerances. Also, I will program the diagnostic computer to register the static and warn us far before it fries anything again."

"That is a relief," Joy replied, her voice calmer. "You are right. As much as NASA can run a million simulations, check and doublecheck parts, there is just no way to ensure how they will function other than watching them function and sometimes fail. We are just lucky we have a great crew."

"Blessed by the stars ma'am," Havoc agreed. "Do we have any other matters that need attending to?"

"Not that I can think of or listed on my agenda," Joy replied. "I understand that things have been tense and not exactly ideal. Make use of Sam's psychology programming and try to calm your minds. Though we cannot guarantee smooth sailing, you will need to be level headed should it not be the case."

"Agreed," Havoc replied. "This is Havoc signing off."

"Mission control signing off," Joy replied before Sam's face went back to normal.

"So, what is it?" Havoc said as he turned to Aiko and smiled. "What is on your mind?"

"Am I that transparent?" Aiko said with a nervous laugh.

"It is my job to know my crew," Havoc replied. "What is troubling you?"

"There was another interruption in the module on Mars," Aiko replied. "I was going to start analyzing it when all this happened."

Havoc nodded. "Am I right to assume you would find investigating the signal more desirable than some downtime?"

"You do know me quite well," Aiko agreed.

"Then do it," Havoc replied. "Get Coz to help you if you need it. Tell him I approved it."

Aiko nodded. "Thank you, Captain. I will start working on this at once."

"Come to me before you tell anything to mission control," Havoc replied. "Depending on what you discover, it might have to be handled and phrased just right. This could be sabotage. It could be interference. It could be something else. If we want to have a say in how mission control wants this handled, we will need to control the narrative."

"I agree," Aiko said with a nod before leaving the cabin. "I will figure this out one way or the other … I hate unanswered questions."

Later in Aiko's lab, Coz and Sam prepared with Aiko to begin their investigation to the second interruption.

"So, you want to brief me to what we already know?" Coz asked.

"Well, as mentioned, there was an interruption with our link to one of the modules already on Mars," Aiko summarized. "We were able to discover that something was broadcasting a signal exactly like the one it was sending and cancelling it out. The likelihood that was from Earth was small."

"Right," Coz replied. "And we lost contact with it again, right before the engine failure?"

"Yes and no," Sam replied. "We did notice an event, but it is more complicated."

"Yes and no?" Coz scoffed. "You are a machine Sam. Doesn't your world rest on something being one way or another?"

"You speak of binary?" Sam asked. "The basic programing of machines that is either off or on … zero or one?"

"Yes," Coz replied. "That is how computers work."

"Most traditional computers," Sam replied. "My brain is not most computers."

"You must excuse me, Sam," Coz replied. "My specialties are physics, chemistry, and biology. I am not an engineer."

"Well, quantum computers have the ability to consider more than two outcomes to any question," Sam replied. "We consider the yes and the no, but also the certain and uncertain … in this way we can fully understand the quite complex state known as maybe."

"How does this relate to the module?" Aiko asked as she looked at her tablet. "The computer is saying that it was offline for the same amount of time as the last time."

"The computer is not a quantum computer," Sam replied. "It is the much more reliable system of … is or is not. The computer was told to keep in contact with the module and alert us of any interruption. As it went to check, the module did not respond so it classified it as offline. However, it was not offline … it was just mostly so."

"Mostly so?" Coz asked. "So, it was blocking the signal enough to confuse the connection but not as powerful as the last time?"

"Basically," Sam replied. "The last time was when the signals were the same and that caused the interruption. This time the signal was about ninety percent the same."

"What about the other ten percent?" Aiko asked. "Was it just a weaker signal?"

"No," Sam replied. "The signal was the same strength as last time. It was like someone said a phrase, and the anomaly repeated it. This time the phrase was said and the anomaly repeated it but changed a couple of letters."

"Isolate the ten percent they changed," Aiko commented. "Analyze."

"You are referring to a they," Coz asked. "Do you mean people on Earth or … something else?"

"Well, we kind of ruled out a signal from Earth," Aiko replied. "We are sure that this signal is neither from Earth or from this ship."

"Therefore, it had to come from Mars," Coz asked. "So how do we see if this signal and its change are random or deliberate?"

"Well, that depends on what the errant part of the signal is," Aiko replied. "If it is simply noise or a distortion, then it could be random. I was just talking to Havoc about some of the components of this ship being subject to factors that would not have shown up in testing or simulation. Though it is very unlikely, based on my understanding of the machines, there is a chance that some other natural factor has caused this to happen."

"What is the deliberation?" Coz asked. "What is the difference between random and patterned in this case?"

"Well, look at it like only radio waves," Aiko added. "The signals would intersect with other signals on similar frequencies. My grandfather used to tell me of times when they used aerial televisions and sometimes you would get part of one channel and part of another. In this case, the errant code could be from another device. We would see the isolated errant pattern as being similar to something else. For example, it could be part of a signal from another device. There are mostly three options. One is that the errant part is just garbage and random. Two, that the signal is part of another signal and just over-lapping. Three, someone mimicked our signal last time and this time is changing a little to see if we notice."

"To see if we notice?" Coz asked in shock. "That would imply that something on the other end is cognizant we are coming."

"Not necessarily," Aiko replied. "It is more likely something simplistic as if they are aware that we do in fact exist."

"Well then, that leads to the opposite that they too exist," Coz replied. "Which is probably the biggest revelation here. That there is a they."

"Well, that remains to be proven or not," Aiko added as she turned back to Sam on the diagnostic table. "What do we have?"

"Upon first scan, the computer and I thought the errant signal was random," Sam replied. "But there was something off about it. Using the system, I told you about before … I thought that maybe it was something else. I had been going under the assumption that all the ten percent of errant signal was singular. I fed it through again, seeing if all or part was something. What I came up with is that nine percent of the errant signal is gibberish, a patch of code that could come from a myriad of issues. However, the last one percent … that is interesting."

"Interesting," Coz asked. "Is it complicated?"

"Far from it," Sam replied. "It is only a thirty-four-digit code."

"Put it on screens," Aiko replied.

The screen lit up behind Sam, displaying the code.

2753164253142312112132413524613572

"Shit," Coz replied, his face turning white.

"I am not sure I see it yet," Aiko admitted.

"You need to break it up," Coz replied. "The first four digits are a set, then the next four is that number but each digit one less. It eventually counts down to nothing then restarts half-way as the digits ramp up to the original four. See the last four digits are the same as the first but backwards."

"It's a pattern!" Aiko replied. "It descends in a non-random way then ascends again in the exact same manner."

"Precisely," Coz admitted. "If you had to communicate to someone whose language and procedures you had no way to understand, you would use math. Math is universal to all those who understand it."

"But the question remains," Sam interjected. "What are they saying?"

"I would imagine they aren't saying anything complicated," Coz replied. "In this case, I would guess it is something akin to … we noticed that you noticed us."

Aiko leaned back in her chair. She sighed and ran her fingers through her hair.

"I really do not know how to reconcile this?"

"What part?" Coz asked. "The fact that we just proved there is an intelligent … something on Mars? Or the fact that this might greatly complicate things?"

"Both," Aiko admitted. "And so much more."

***

The group was gathered in the utility room, a large compartment useable for all manner of experiments and projects. Everyone assembled looking either curious or mad that they were being pulled away from other matters. As Havoc joined the group, everyone looked up as if things were going to get started.

"Thank you everyone for coming," Havoc said with a nod. "This conversation is off record and what we decide to do is based on an agreement."

Ivy looked to Havoc with a skeptical expression.

"You seem so serious. Have we had another malfunction? Is there anything to be worried about?"

"Far from it," Havoc replied. "In fact, this is likely one of the greatest moments of recent scientific history."

"I don't understand," Ivy replied. "What could have happened out here in the last few hours?"

"We found … something," Aiko added. "Something intelligent."

"On Mars." Aiko added. "Ahead of us."

"Something has been messing with one of the modules already on Mars," Coz replied. "I can tell you the whole thing, but to make a long story short, something or some … one on Mars mimicked one of our signals to basically say 'hi'."

"Actually, hello or something like hello?" Prof asked. "For both have a very big difference."

"Well, not exactly hi," Aiko added. "But the general sense is to show us that they exist."

"Do we have a contingency for this?" Mack asked, seeming unaffected by the monumental thing they were just told. "I mean, we have contingencies for if a case of whooping cough breaks out up here. You're telling me we don't have one for that?"

"You would be surprised," Havoc replied. "It is a thing that we don't."

"I always figured that when I joined NASA, I would get all the secrets to the little green men," Coz replied. "But, alas, none were to be found … well other than potentially this one."

"This is something NASA would keep quite a tight lid on," Havoc admitted. "With all the conspiracy theories and strange occurrences, the ups and downs of NASA, they would not tell us anything we didn't need to know. That said … if they knew there was something waiting for us on Mars, I can guarantee you that I would be the one to have a contingency for it."

"They love keeping a lid on stuff like this," Coz commented. "Though I wish there was more information for us. We potentially have Marvin waiting for us with no real knowledge on what to do about it."

"War of the worlds," Prof replied. "That is why they are so silent."

"An actual war of the worlds?" Mack asked. "The supposed idea that we are already being visited by aliens? I don't buy it."

"Not the conspiracies, Mack," Prof replied. "I am speaking of the radio play."

"The one by Orson Wells?" Ivy asked. "The one that scared people?"

"Exactly," Prof replied. "Conspiracies, sightings in the sky, it is all a mess of fakes and hearsay. However, you want to see a real situation of the world at large dealing with this information … that is the best case. It is like a double-blind experiment where a large test group did not know reality from fantasy."

"Did they really not know?" Aiko asked. "I have heard of it and it seems strange to me that such a large amount of people fell for a radio play."

"Well, you are of the generation to grow up with realistic effects in movies and television," Prof replied, swiping on a tablet for pictures of things from movies. "You think of an alien and you think of comic book battles in space or monstrous super beings. However, back in the day there was nothing but imagination. They had no way to be desensitized to what they heard."

Sam lit up and rotated, simulating looking at the others. "According to the investigations after the fact, it was a perfect accident. At the beginning of the war of the worlds broadcast, they say very clearly it is a play. However, at the time people were tuned to a different program. It was not until an interlude that they changed the channel and got to the program where it was mimicking a news broadcast. This was right before world war two when such broadcasts were a primary source of information."

"Pre-internet," Coz said with a laugh. "Dark times."

"We are getting way off topic here," Havoc replied.

"Not really," Prof replied. "The point that I was making that when a large amount of people is faced with a very convincing report of life from the stars, they panic and it cause a wide out chaos. The fact that it was fake is moot as the people reacted naturally to the stimulus."

"You think if what we found gets out, it will cause the same issue?" Ivy asked. "How will it get past all the hearsay and chaff to be taken seriously?"

"We are not some crackpot in a comic shop spreading UFO sightings," Prof replied. "We are a multi-trillion-dollar vessel carrying the first human beings to another world. The Earth is looking at us and anything that we find will be taken VERY seriously."

"So that leads us back to what we do," Havoc replied. "Because, as I mentioned, there is no contingency for it."

"I remember reading about a book where a bunch of scientists were assembled to figure out first contact," Ivy offered.

"The one where they go to the bottom of the ocean?" Coz asked. "I liked that one."

"Can we be serious here?" Havoc replied. "Sam, what would you suggest."

"Well, I would think this is not as big of a dilemma as you are suggesting," Sam replied in his analytic tone. "You are, by definition, space explorers. If ever a group was to be assembled to answer the question of first contact, it would be you. Since this indeed might be the first contact with life outside of Earth, it would take the same adaptability and problem solving you all are trained for. The fact of the matter is that though we know for a fact there is something there, we have extremely little information as to the what. So, the question cannot be how to deal with it … because until we get there, we have no way to know what we will find. The issue is what do we do about it in relation to mission control."

"Yeah," Coz nodded. "They are really antsy, dealing with the cyber-attack and the threat of protests. We tell them that there is an unknown variable ahead of us, they will turn us around faster than a stressed-out parent on their way to the mall with their kids."

"Should we be keeping something like this a secret?" Ivy replied. "What if it is dangerous?"

"What if it's not?" Prof replied. "Do you want to turn away from being the first to discover one of the greatest discoveries of mankind because mission control has an itchy cancel button finger?"

"We have been training so hard," Mack replied. "We are over seventy five percent of the way there. Turning back now literally erases what we have worked so hard for."

"We do not even know the complexity of what it is," Coz added. "It could be like someone looking around at Earth and a mockingbird replied the beeps on the probe. Would it make sense to turn back?"

"It is some pretty complex math though," Havoc replied. "Nothing an animal can do."

"How do we know what animals on Mars could do?" Ivy broke in.

"We just learned that there might BE animals on Mars like ten minutes ago."

Aiko was quiet. She knew a lot about machines and technology, but these debates were not something she wanted to engage in. She preferred simple ideas, ones that took a complex idea and boiled it down to its most primal problem. This is how she found her solutions. Havoc seemed to notice this pause and lack of speaking and interrupted the group.

"Aiko," Havoc asked. "What do you think we should do?"

Everyone stopped, seeming to say, since it was she that discovered it, that maybe it's her call.

"Well, the issue is not if we should tell mission control," Aiko replied. "Because we most definitely have to. The thing should be when."

"What do you mean?" Coz asked.

"Well, we don't know anything now, really," Aiko replied. "We are sitting here faced with literally all we have uncovered and we can't figure it out. Imagine what mission control would do with their outsider-looking-in approach. They will look at it as a keep going or turn back thing. We need a situation that takes this choice away from them without making it look like we did."

"We can't be turned around if we are there," Mack added. "We hold off to get more information. When we land on Mars we tell them we might have something. They cannot so easily abort and we buy time to figure it out."

"Works for me," Havoc replied. "Anyone else want to weigh in on this plan?"

"I am a man of science," Coz replied. "I prefer to keep my results to myself until I have gone through the full experiment."

"I agree," Ivy added. "It seems so small a view to base a judgment on at this time."

"I will do whatever you deem best, Captain," Mack replied. "I trust your judgment."

"Prof?" Havoc said while turning to the large doctor. "We have to be unanimous."

"I'm in," Prof nodded. "The idea of new life fascinates me."

"Ok, that leaves Sam," Havoc replied as he turned to the spherical robot.

"I do not count," Sam replied. "I do what I am told by Engineer Aiko and you Captain Havoc."

"I know you are but a program," Havoc said with a smile. "But Aiko is not the only one here that regards you as a friend. I want your opinion and will count it as much as any member of the crew."

"Well I would say my feelings on the matter are more based on curiosity than anything else," Sam replied. "I would imagine that should we turn around, we will not get another chance to get a signal. So, my vote is to go with the others."

"Then it is settled," Havoc replied. "We withhold information about the … contact from NASA until either we know more about it that signals a problem or we get to Mars."

"I think we should keep our ears peeled for more anomalies," Coz replied. "To see if they speak again."

"There is one thing we did not discuss," Aiko added. "It sent a number series to tell us it was there. Should we respond that we heard it?"

"That would be the best way to illicit more information on the subject," Sam replied. "It was mimicking our connection signal to communicate, changing a small part of it. We could easily to the same."

"How?" Havoc replied.

"Well, it made a set of specific numbers showing us a descending and ascending pattern," Aiko added. "We just add one that ascends then descends. It shows that we both found it and understood it."

Havoc sighed. "Anyone object to this?"

Everyone remained silent, all seemingly excited for the idea of the first response to an alien signal.

Havoc nodded. "Do it. Let me know the moment you get any kind of response."

"We will," Aiko nodded, already forming how to do it in her head. Things were about to get much more exciting and Aiko could barely contain herself.

**

Aiko sat in the large pod. She could not it differentiate from a tanning booth. She had been in there only a few minutes but it felt like it had been an hour. Though no one would call the giant spinning tubes of the ship spacious and she was not exactly claustrophobic, there was something about the small chamber she did not like.

"You know I think this is my least favorite part about space travel," Aiko commented, knowing Prof was next to the tube. "Do we really need tans in space?"

"Everyone seems to think this thing is a tanning booth," Prof said with a laugh. "Did you know I helped invent this thing?"

"Really?" Aiko asked. "Then you tell me how it is not a tanning booth."

"The human body is accustomed to a certain amount of exposure to the sun," Prof explained. "It keeps you healthy and gives you much needed vitamins. Since going outside this place to expose your skin to the sun is … problematic … an alternative needed to be found. We have simulated gravity and exercise routines to keep your body in shape. This is to keep your skin in shape."

"If you say so," Aiko replied. "I did not let much let sun hit my skin before I left Earth. I spent a lot of my time in labs and underground."

"Well, then add fixing your bad health habits to the benefits of this machine," Prof added.

"I know, I know," Aiko replied. "I suppose I am just complaining for complaining sake."

"So, let's talk about something else," Prof replied as he began to tap on a tablet. "Any return from the signal we sent back to the … them?"

"Not so far," Aiko admitted, it had been three weeks since she had sent the signal back through the machine and so far, nothing had come back. "I can only assume that it might take them longer to decipher our response as we did to decipher their original message."

"I understand your frustration," Prof replied. "When we all discussed the anomaly, it seemed so exciting and new. I suppose we all assumed that we would get more immediate discoveries. Such is the way this kind of thing works I suppose."

"In what way?" Aiko asked.

"Well, when we look at historical events in hindsight, they seem so exciting," Prof explained. "A myriad of events, each a part of a puzzle leading up to great discovery or world changing event. They took much longer with missteps, doubt and diverging paths. I am sure the people doing it did not see it quite as fast and exciting as the people reading about it afterwards."

"I suppose you are right," Aiko replied. "Though I am more of a person that focus' on a problem or invention on a linear path until it is done. I am not used to stopping and waiting."

"Well, that is because you have no means of distraction," Prof replied. "You just focus, focus, focus."

"I suppose I need a distraction," Aiko replied.

Lights began to flicker. The solar bed's light going up and down. Warning lights began to beep.

"Be careful what you ask for," Prof said as he hit an intercom button. "Is everything alright?"

The intercom blared as if to speak and all the lights in the room suddenly went out. Seconds later emergency lights came on.

"Aiko, I think we are done," Prof replied as he walked over to the solar bed and slowly opened it manually.

"I think you are right," Aiko said as she walked over to the intercom. She paused, feeling the deck with her bare feet. "Main power is out."

"How do you know?" Prof responded. "All the screens are off."

"I can feel it," Aiko replied. "The ship has a natural vibration from the main power generators. I can feel the outer ring affected."

"Will we stop spinning?" Prof asked. "Will we lose gravity? Will we lose air?"

"Things that spin in space want to keep spinning," Aiko replied as she tried to get a tablet up and running. It seemed to have been re-set and she struggled to use the backups to get it back online. "The ship is designed so the spinning outer section will power the oxygen reclaimer and keep it working in case of engine failure. However, the generators do cause friction and the ring will eventually slow. At that time, we lose air and gravity."

"How long?" Prof asked. "How long until gravity is an issue and the air starts to thin?"

"Forty-five minutes," Aiko replied, seeing her tablet come online good as new. "It looks like we had some sort of electromagnetic event. Everything here is shielded to back itself up but it will need to be reset."

"Well, do it then!" Prof replied, seeming to be more than a little concerned.

"I can't do it from here," Aiko explained. "I need your help. I am going to get Sam, reset him if needed and get to the core. I want you to find the others and take them to the bridge. I will try and get bridge power up first."

"Why the bridge?" Prof replied. "Should we not discuss this with the captain?"

"The bridge is the escape vehicle," Aiko replied. "In the case of catastrophic failure, that is where everyone should be. As we cannot contact everyone now, that is procedure."

"What about you?" Prof responded. "Should you not come with us?"

"No," Aiko replied as she used the manual release to open the hospital module door. "It is my job to save the ship if I can."

Aiko moved though the ship. Though the change in the gravity at this point was incredibly minor she could feel the difference. She knew that she would eventually be working in zero G once she got to the core and wanted to do as much as she could before then. She used the manual override to get to the lab and opened it. She expected to see everything off, but, instead, most of the automated machines were still on and acting erratically. She went around them, not having time to deal with anything non-essential now and focusing on what was necessary. She saw Sam, in his cradle, his eyes flashing on and off.

"Come on Sam, I am going to need you here," Aiko replied. "I have never had to reset you."

"Red What Orange," Sam replied, his voice devoid of simulated tone. "Horse Charlie You Vector Black."

"Ok, you are solid state so I can't just turn you on and off," Aiko replied. "I need to trigger some sort of automated program to force your system to reboot itself."

Aiko stood for a moment, just staring at Sam.

"Durango Are Dallas," Sam continued. "Green Hello Delta."

Aiko moved her hand around Sam's visual input and found, thought it was flashing, it was still reacting to motion.

"Ok, you are aware I am here but you are too jumbled from the electromagnetic shock. What is something hardwired you cannot ignore? Keep the ship running ... well that's not really doing it ... protect the crew ... wait!"

Sam just continued to flutter around, seemingly aware of stimulus but unable to respond.

"Sorry to do this Sam," Aiko said as she stepped back and picked up a screwdriver from the table and looked at it. She placed the flat end against her jugular. "Normally I would not play around with this kind of thing."

Sam did not react, his eyes still flashing, but he stopped talking the gibberish tones.

"Ok," Aiko said as she took a deep breath and prepared her best dramatic tone. "I am in extreme distress and I feel that I might hurt myself."

Sam paused, his eyes stopping flickering for a moment, then going back to flashing.

"I am serious!" Aiko replied. "I cannot take this cruel universe anymore!"

"W-w-what," Sam replied. "What made you feel this way Engineer Aiko?"

"Sam you're back!" Aiko replied, dropping the screwdriver and walking over to the cradle.

"My systems are still a bit of a mess I am afraid," Sam replied. "Though I am repairing them as we talk. Very smart, using my hardwired need to protect the crew to reset my core system."

"I like to think I have some good ideas," Aiko replied. "I need your help and I need it fast."

"What is going on?" Sam asked. "I am not able to communicate with the main computer … I will begin resetting systems. Is main power offline?"

"It is," Aiko replied. "The outer ring is beginning to slow. It is going to get lighter in here, and a lot colder very soon."

"I will start to reset the ship systems," Sam replied. "But you will need to reset the core manually."

"I know," Aiko replied. "Start resetting the ship. Start with the bridge. That is where everyone is."

"Not everyone," Mack said as they came through the door. "Everyone else is there and I am here to help in any way I can."

"It isn't safe," Aiko said as she gathered her tools and prepared to leave. "The ship is the escape pod."

"An escape pod with two pilots," Mack replied. "Figured you could use a hand."

"I will handle the rest of the ships systems," Sam replied, though if you don't get that core running again, they won't stay on very long."

Aiko nodded before turning to Mack. "Ok, come with me. Do you have any engineering training?"

"None," Mack replied as they followed Aiko though the ship toward the connectors to the central section of the ship. "But I have displayed an amazing capacity for pressing the buttons I am told to press."

"Good enough," Aiko replied, manually opening the connection lock and going through, shifting from earth gravity to zero gravity. "There are going to be a lot of buttons."

"Outstanding," Mack replied.

Aiko used the installed bars along the capsule to fly though, she went deeper and deeper into the craft. With Mack's help Aiko was more easily able to get the manual door releases open and soon found their way to the core.

"Is it off?" Mack asked. "Isn't it like a reactor?"

"It is never off technically," Aiko said as she began to go through some checks. "As a hybrid fusion generator, it literally generates its own power and is shielded from any electromagnetic anomalies. However, to protect it, should the ship experience a failure such as this the system is designed to automatically cut it off."

"Then what is the big problem?" Mack asked. "If this is what it was supposed to do can't we just switch it back on?"

"Hopefully," Aiko said as she began to manually reset some of the switches. "The issue is that though it is designed to cut itself off to prevent shutdown and explosion it has been proven problematic to reconnect it."

"Define problematic?" Mack asked.

"Well, they ran a series of simulations about core disconnects and reconnects," Aiko replied, pointing to a lever behind Mack that needed to be thrown. "In the simulations, it only came back on sixty percent of the time."

"And the other times?" Mack replied as they threw the lever.

"The system went dead and the core eventually melted down," Aiko replied.

"That does not seem like an ideal response to a simulation," Mack replied. "Especially for something that we need to like … you know … live."

"You would be surprised how many things on this ship were passed in what they refer to as acceptable risk," Aiko replied. "The realities of space travel. I had a rather disturbing discussion on expendability with Havoc during our last disaster."

"I am in the Air Force, Aiko," Mack replied. "They teach us about acceptable losses and expendability on day one."

"Well, let's hope we beat the odds then," Aiko replied. "I think I got all of the core breakers ready to go. Sam, you got the computer online yet?"

"Yes, Engineer Aiko," Sam replied through the comm system. "All essential systems online at least."

"Ok," Aiko agreed. "Mack and I are about to reset the connection to the core. Warn the bridge that there is about to be a lurch as the ring turbines power back up … if in two minutes they don't feel it … tell them … better just tell them to brace."

Mack braced themselves and readied to flip the last switches indicated by Aiko. "I'm ready."

Aiko grabbed a hold of a bar by the core. "Do it!"

Mack flipped the switch, nothing happening. "That is bad, right?"

Aiko paused, a few seconds passing and there was a rumbling sound through the ship and lights around the core went to light up. "No! Everything is powering back up!"

"I guess it is an acceptable margin," Mack replied with a smile as the ship lurched and made them grip the bracings tightly. "At least this time."

"Sam how are we looking?" Aiko asked.

"Main power coming back online and the main computer is getting the ring back up to optimal running speed. We should be alright."

"Good," Aiko replied. "Contact the bridge and tell them that all is fine and we are not dying today."

"Will do," Sam replied. "Coz is going to love that phrasing."

***

The event with the power down was over seemingly before anything truly bad could happen. The ship was in a period of straight course so even had it not been powered down, the engines did not need to fire. It took only a few minutes to get main power back on line and about another day to get every little system online and free of bugs. There was a lot of corrupted data and blown out systems, but nothing that did not have a backup. Aiko and Coz spent two weeks going over all of it before the ship could be considered back to full shape. The exact cause was unknown, but from what all sensors said that it was an electromagnetic spike from a sunspot that hit the ship at the worst angle at the exact wrong time. Telemetry from NASA confirmed the spike and thought it did nothing on Earth it caused disruption with many satellites and long range transceivers. The Earth was relatively lucky, with its thick atmosphere, most of the radiation from the sun was filtered out and it protected those below. Though the ship was radiation shielded, it seemingly was not quite prepared for a blast of that magnitude and it is what called the problem. Many of the crew remained antsy, but mission control assured the crew that the chances of getting hit again were a hundred million to one. The math indeed made Aiko more relived, but certain members of the crew did not take it as the same relief.

There was a thought that NASA would turn the ship around after the shutdown, but they seemed to think that since the ship was only offline for a few moments and it was not that much of a problem. The idea that they did not want to turn around for being so close stayed heavily on their minds and everyone could only really focus on looking forward.

Aiko spent as much time as she could check and recheck every affected system. Though others seemed to be ok with the fact that a random space event almost crippled the ship, she was not. The idea that there was no way to foresee issues like that was no solace against Aiko's efforts to be ready for anything. One morning, just as she was planning a new series of diagnostics she received a call from Havoc.

"Aiko to the bridge please," Havoc asked.

"Can it wait?" Aiko replied. "I am about to set todays maintenance timetable?"

"I guarantee that it cannot," Havoc replied. "We are all up here."

Aiko sighed. She had not slept well the night before and wanted to give the captain grief for pulling her away from her work … routine and redundant or not. However, as she opened the door to the bridge she saw something that made her speechless. Past her crew, past the front porthole was an orb of orangey red, almost completely filling the field of view.

"My friends and comrades," Havoc said proudly. "May I present Mars?"

"We are here?" Aiko asked. "I thought we were still a few days out."

"You have been burying yourself in your work Aiko," Sam replied from his bridge cradle. "We have been updating everyone in the daily briefings."

"Every daily briefing has said how close we are to Mars," Aiko admitted with a laugh. "I stopped reading that part a while ago."

"Moving toward Mars and preparing to fire thrusters to plot synchronous orbit," Mack spoke up. "In about twenty minutes we will officially be orbiting Mars."

"Start ticking off firsts," Coz replied. "First humans in orbit of another planet, first humans to go down … there will be a bunch of firsts and all with our names."

"The first of many," Ivy replied. "We hopefully will have a new home for humanity here."

"True, but we will be the first," Coz replied. "Everyone remember Neil Armstrong and Buzz Aldrin. Their names taught to children as early as elementary school. No one talks about the subsequent people. Even that mission five years back to build that transceiver on the moon ... I can't recall a single name on that team."

Havoc laughed. "Mack was on that mission."

"No shit?" Coz replied. "When did you become a pilot? When you were twelve?"

"Fourteen," Mack replied. "Air Force at eighteen and NASA by twenty."

"We are all the best of our fields," Prof replied. "Well, maybe most of us ... what is it you do again Coz?"

"Very funny," Coz replied. "I might not fly trillion dollar spaceships but once we get down there ... it is my job to turn that red ball into Earth's bitch."

"The language you spout sometimes," Ivy said with a laugh. "Though I suppose we are literally arriving at another planet, such things should not be unexpected."

"Ok," Havoc said as he strapped into a chair next to Mack. "Now that the excitement is over, we have some work to do. Feel free to stay on the bridge, but you will have to strap in. This is not the bumpy part, but there will be some potential G-forces as we fire the rockets to slow down."

One by one, people began to strap themselves in. Mack and Havoc went through complicated procedures and Aiko could feel the ship rumbling as the engines were doing the opposite of that they have been doing for months.

"Engineer Aiko," Sam stated in a calm tone. "I know this is an inopportune time, but we are receiving an interruption from the module below."

"Now?" Aiko asked.

"Yes now," Sam replied. "Though I would imagine that whoever is interfering cannot tell how far we are from the transceiver and proximity is receiving the signal very fast. It is recycling now and I think I can begin the analysis."

"Don't mind if you take care of that now." Havoc replied. "But as of now it is not the best time to do it here."

Aiko nodded, taking Sam out of his cradle and taking her back to her lab. She set him on his terminal and powered up her tablet.

"What do we have," Aiko asked, her curiosity barely able to be contained.

"Another errant signal," Sam replied. "This one is not taking much more space, but is about twenty percent different than our message."

"What does it say?" Aiko replied, looking over the coded signal on her own device but not able to decipher it.

"It is very curious," Sam replied. "The codes seem to correspond to letters."

"Letters?" Aiko replied. "As in a human alphabet?"

"Indeed," Sam replied. "It appears as though this signal has some manner of our language and alphabet."

"Well, what does it say?" Aiko replied, her heart skipping a beat.

"More like what do they ask," Sam replied. "The message is simply ... are you still there?"

"Still?" Aiko replied. "That is kind of a big thing. The fact that they are saying still denotes that there is a reason why we might not be here. I mean, a big question is how they accessed our language or can figure it out. However, the biggest question is that they would have some reason to think we were not still here."

"Well, it would seem to indicate there was a message we missed," Sam replied.

"But we didn't miss anything," Aiko pondered as she swiped though logs on her pad. "The module is the only way we have to contact them and we have been monitoring it very closely."

"That is true," Sam replied. "Though there is something that has eluded notice."

"We don't miss things," Aiko pondered, an idea beginning to form in her head. "Unless they had very bad timing."

"What do you mean Engineer Aiko?" Sam asked.

"Well, according to our recollection there should be three interruptions," Aiko replied. "Do an analysis on the signal from the module and tell me how many interruptions we have experienced, from this errant signal or otherwise."

"Four," Sam relied. "One being the power outage from the solar flare."

"Exactly!" Aiko replied. "What if they tried to send us a signal at the precise moment we got the solar flare?"

"Unlikely, but not impossible," Sam replied. "Though I would have no way to look at the information. All telemetry from remote modules was scrambled and not properly recorded during the outage."

"Not necessarily," Aiko replied. "The machines were acting erratically during the flare. What if the signal came in, our computer prioritized it like we told it to but it got jumbled in the noise."

"Still," Sam replied. "I have no record of the time before my cognizance reset.

"Well, if there had been a signal, you would have looked into it, immediately right?" Aiko asked. "There's a good chance you were downloading the information from the module at the time of the event."

"Indeed, I would have accessed it immediately," Sam replied. "But the problem remains that even if I was connected to the information from the module, I would have no way to recall it."

"You were saying strange things," Aiko recalled. "Seemingly gibberish words and it could be part of what you were doing when you were hit."

"I have no way to recall what I said," Sam replied. "I am sorry."

"But I remember it," Aiko replied. "I have an erratic Eidetic memory. I cannot always control it, but I remember what you said while you were in your crashed state."

"That is rather impressive," Sam replied. "What is it?"

Aiko took a breath, letting her mind act like a reflex as she blurted out the information. "Red What Orange Horse Charlie You Vector Black Durango Are Dallas Green Hello Delta."

"Very curious," Sam replied. "The technical code to access remote systems on Mars is speech translated as Red Orange Horse Charlie Vector Black Durango Dallas Green Delta."

"There were other words in there though," Aiko replied. "What You Are Hello."

"I would imagine it is more likely the following," Sam offered. "Hello, what are you?"

"That does sound like the most reasonable question an intelligence would have for another it just discovered," Aiko replied, her heart racing. "They likely sent out that signal in response to our mathematic answer to theirs. Would they have gotten anything back if they sent it just as the flare hit?"

"Likely heavy feedback," Sam replied. "It might have seemed to them as if something bad had happened."

"Hence the question of if we are still here," Aiko agreed. "But how did they learn our language?"

"They might not know much of it," Sam replied. "Questions like what are you and are you still there are well within the automated questions the standard operating system on the module I know. I would imagine, for example, they know things like us, them, here, there, now, then, what when and why. They have the basic syntax of our language but not much of the meaning."

"Should we respond?" Aiko replied. "To both questions?"

"That is really up to you," Sam replied. "As stated, there is no actual procedure to responding to first contact and the captain has left this in your hands."

"Ok, I want you to respond," Aiko nodded. "Tell them simply … we are friends and we are here."

***

The ship slowed down from its accelerated speed and went into orbit of Mars with no issues. Mission control was contacted and an air of relief and celebration spread throughout the crew. Aiko decided that she would wait until asked as there was a lot of work to be done. Though she had no real part to play during the orbital maneuver, there was much to do for the landing. First up was to lock down everything in her lab for the landing and make sure there were no technical issues to report that might interfere with the landing. Once she gave the all clear there was a bigger problem … getting some sleep.

For hours, Aiko was awake in her bunk. Ideas of setting foot on Mars and the strange intelligence would not go silent in her mind. There was so much ahead to discover and she could literally not wait to discover it. She did manage to finally get a couple hours, but by the time she got to the bridge and strapped in for the decent, she was jittery and filled with nerves.

"Hello everyone on mission control," Havoc said to the comm, knowing his words likely were being broadcast worldwide on Earth. "We are but moments away from starting our decent to the surface of Mars. We have done a full orbit and managed to position ourselves on an angle that will lead to the base that was already set up by remote. The decent will only take about ten minutes, but we will be out of communication for that time. NASA will still be able to track our progress, but non-essential systems like direct communication will be temporarily offline. So, I am going to sign off for now to make the decent and speak to you when we are on Mars."

"Make us proud," Joy replied from the other end of the line. "Talk to you soon."

Havoc switched off the comm. "Everyone check stations. I am about to initiate the descent."

"All systems are go captain," Aiko replied. "Unless anyone has any objections I am giving you the all clear."

No one said anything and Havoc turned back to his controls and nodded to Mack. "Let's do it."

The engines rumbled and the ship began to move toward the planet. Within seconds the ship began to rumble violently and heat began to light up as the friction of the atmosphere encountered the shielded hull of the ship. Though the atmosphere was thinner than Earth, it still caused friction and was a challenge that needed to be overcome. Aiko kept her eyes glued to her panel. She admitted that space travel was not so bad, but the flying in planets gravity was not so much fun. This was the time where a small error could mean catastrophic problems and likely faster than she could fix it. All she could do is keep looking at her readouts, as long as they stayed in the green, all was fine. Aiko knew that though she was instrumental to getting them here, this was Mack and Havoc's game. This was their time to shine and everyone's fate was in their hands. Though she was surrounded by danger and uncertainty, her trust of Mack and Havoc gave her reason to relax, is just for a little.

Unlike many space vessels, the ship was not designed to break up in orbit and leave things behind. It was painstakingly developed to close in on itself and take everything with it to set up a base on Mars. A module below that was like a crane would assemble the vessel from space ship to Mars base.

Mack was at the controls and, once through the upper atmosphere, went into precise maneuvers to slow down the ship and make it exactly to the landing pad. Havoc worked as the co-pilot. Though he had more experience and training, even he admitted Mack's skills were better than his. Aiko respected the man's humility and his faith in the skills of those who served him.

Aiko lost track of the moves, the maneuver, the G-forces growing greater and lesser to greater again. Soon there was a strong thud and then there were no forces at all except for a pull backwards to the rear of the cabin.

"Are we here?" Coz asked, opening his eyes that had been seemingly closed the entire time.

"Welcome to Mars," Mack replied, flipping switches on their console. "Changing to landed configuration."

"The ship moved forward, powerful arms in the landed module lowering the ship and beginning the task of disassembling it and re-assembling it. Over the next hour, the crew waited patiently as the module did exactly what it was supposed to and connected the ship to other parts on the ground and their ship joined a massive facility already in place.

Soon the group got out of their seats and headed back into the vessel. It was so strange for all of them. All of their labs, all of their facilities were still there, but now, part of a much more massive structure. Instead of a central pillar, there was now a large central building with the original core of the ship in the middle.

The crew met in the now spacious central meeting area. Havoc moved around, seeming to be enjoying the lesser gravity.

"Well, we did it people. Though I am sure you are all a bit overwhelmed, there is the matter of NASA and mission controls broadcast. I am sure they are stalling as much as they can, but there is something that everyone wants to see."

"They want us to set foot on Mars," Ivy replied. "Well foot outside of the facility."

"Exactly," Havoc replied. "This is a rather expensive enterprise and if we cannot get the people excited about it, they might not keep doing it."

"Then we better put on a show," Coz agreed. "Are we doing a surface walk?"

"Indeed," Havoc replied. "The first order of business is to assemble a three-person crew and walk the perimeter of the base to make sure all is where it should be. There is no coincidence of it being prioritized and part of the broadcast. Mission control has been updating then to the fact that we landed but once we get our suits on we are to reconnect with video."

"My recording rig is ready to go," Sam said as he rolled up on a portable rig with three multidirectional wheels and a long tripod. "I look forward to my expanded role now that I am here."

"You sound excited," Aiko replied. "I like it."

"I am invested in this mission as much as any I imagine," Sam replied.

"So that leads to the issue of who is in this little walkabout and who goes first?" Coz asked. "Can it be any of us?"

"I thought you might ask that and this is a mostly formality," Havoc replied. "Which means that since it is being recorded that any of us can go in this mission. For this I have concocted a random way to choose who it is."

"You going to get Sam to use an algorithm or something?" Ivy asked. "Sounds complicated."

"No, I am in fact going analogue," Havoc said as he lifted a space helmet onto the desk. "Inside are pieces of paper with all of our names … well except for Sam … he has to go regardless."

"As the only sentient AI on this mission I am a first regardless," Sam replied.

"Unless anyone objects we will start picking names," Havoc replied. "First picked is first out. Anyone want to do the honors of picking?"

"I will do it," Prof said as he walked over. "I actually do not care much for who is first so it will be the closest to objective we have."

"Works for me," Coz replied. "I am excited."

Prof nodded and reached into the helmet, withdrawing a folded piece of paper. He unfurled it. "Coz it is you."

"Awesome," Coz said with a grin. "Though I would like to give the honor to Mack."

"Really?" Mack said as they raised an eyebrow to Coz.

"Yes, really," Coz said with a smile. "Mack got us here and … they deserve it."

"Thank you, Coz," Mack said with a smile. "That is very honorable of you."

"Second is me," Prof said as he held up the paper for all to see. "I just hope I don't have to say anything like a speech."

"I got something," Mack replied. "We're good."

"That is a relief," Prof replied. "So, we pick the third and final member of the first excursion on Mars."

Aiko stayed silent. She wanted so much to be chosen but did not want to seem too eager to her colleagues. She watched in almost slow motion as Prof drew the final paper to be opened. She could imagine it being any of the remaining names and could not picture it being hers.

"Aiko," Prof replied. "You are the third."

Aiko sighed in relief, her mind spinning with the implications.

Without further ado, the trio went to the external airlock and put on their spacesuits. They did not use the emergency units and it took some time. However, soon all three stood together in their suits, ready to go and see mars for the first time with human eyes.

"We have Joy and mission control about to go live," Sam replied from his mobile mount. "Is everyone ready to begin?"

"Yes," Mack nodded, turning toward Sam and putting their hand on the control panel on the door for dramatic effect.

"You are live with mission control," Sam replied, a light coming on to focus on what he was filming.

"This is Joy from mission control." Joy replied in an eager voice. The world is watching and we are so excited to see that you have safely landed on the surface of Mars."

"We are about to go out and look at the facility," Mack replied. "This is co-pilot Mack and we drew to see who would go out first. I will go first, followed by medical officer Prof, and our Engineer Aiko."

"That sounds wonderful," Joy replied. "Do any of you have anything to say before you go out?"

"I want to thank everyone who built this ship and all of this wondrous technology," Aiko replied. "It is a wonder of mankind that our creativity and ingenuity literally has transported a group of people to a different planet."

"Well said," Joy agreed. "Prof, have you any words for the world."

"I am not really a man for speeches," Prof replied. "But as we do this thing, we should focus primarily on the fact that we are all one people. This achievement belongs to all of us and it shows the strength we have in unity."

"Excellent point," Joy agreed. "This may have been an effort by a few but it is the triumph of many. "Mack … that leaves you."

"Thank you," Mack replied. "I cannot begin to even reconcile the emotions and feelings inside my head and my heart. But this is a moment that has shown that the dreams of humankind that has looked up at the infinite sky can come true and there is nothing we cannot accomplish."

Mack put their hand on the door controls. The device cycling the air out and opening, revealing a vast sandy red landscape beyond. Sam moved out, his wheels adjusting to the sandy landscape. He went out a few dozen feet then turned back to the group. "I am ready when you are."

"We stand here on the door to infinity," Mack said proudly. "Let's open it and go inside shall we?"

Chapter Three: The Two Knights

The walk on the surface of Mars had been something that Aiko could not have predicted. It was a vast place of striking vistas and vibrant colors. It was like a desert on Earth but with as if it were painted by the gods. The surface walk was mostly ceremonial, with Mack answering questions and talking about how great it was. Aiko was mostly quiet, focusing on the event and burning everything she saw into her mind. They walked around the edge of the base, the massive spaceship parked safely into the core and creating a massive town in space that would serve both as their waystation and the foundation of the next crew to come up and continue what they started. Even with the lessened Mars gravity the spacesuit was still heavy and by the time they did the circuit Aiko's shoulders ached from the suit. She knew it would be a thing she would have to get used to as there would be many, many more surface walks to come.

After that walk and the show was over, the crew settled in to work for what was to come next. Each astronaut had facilities in the ship but were dwarfed by what was shot to Mars before their arrival. Aiko herself now had a massive bay with automated machines to diagnose and service all the tools that would be used on Mars. Aiko dived head first into her massive checklist to make sure that everything was catalogued and working the way it was supposed to.

The lessened gravity took a little getting used to. Aiko was never really a fan of the weightlessness but the outer core of the ship that simulated Earth gravity was something she knew she would miss. Everything felt lighter and though her muscles did not seem to mind she could feel the difference in her head and she did not like it. Prof proscribed daily exercise to keep the muscle density up so it would be easy to readapt to Earth gravity for the return and beyond. Aiko did not even want to think about the return trip. This time, the time now on Mars was her time and she wanted to make the best of it.

As much as Aiko and the rest wanted to see about the module it was not a priority. They had a tight timetable after landing and it took priority. The crew was on the surface of Mars a week before time came to check the module. It was time for scheduled maintenance and checking of the module itself and Aiko found herself excited to do it. She did not expect to see a spaceman standing at the module waiting for her, but she thought that it might lead to some of the answers she so desperately sought.

When it came time to go see the module Coz volunteered to come with her. There was likely no real need for this but the rule was that if you were more than fifty feet from the airlock you had to go in pairs. Aiko's heart raced as she and Coz walked toward the module. Sam followed behind them on one of his movement modules, a set of four multidirectional wheels and a long multipurpose arm. It was not unlike the module which was a massive tripod like machine with massive wheels and a myriad of cultivating arms tucked underneath. It had been used to create the level area for the basecamp but had been mostly idle for months.

"What are we expecting to see?" Coz asked as he walked. "I will admit I was picturing what we might see at the module and came up with nothing."

"I don't think we will see too much," Aiko commented. "The messages were spaced out and sporadic. I doubt whatever was affecting it is just standing around and waiting. Perhaps some kind of patch in equipment."

"We never talked about what would happen if they were hostile," Coz agreed. "This thing might be dangerous … if we have the luck, bad or good, that it is indeed there and waiting."

"There is nothing to indicate that it would be hostile," Aiko replied, spotting the lower area with the interface and beginning to walk around the massive machine. "They seemed more curious than anything, even showing concern that something had happened to us."

"Well they don't have to be intentionally hostile," Coz replied. "Most movies offer on this assumption that life from other worlds is like our own. Even those horror film aliens are most humanoid in shape."

"That is mostly so they can fit an actor in the suit," Sam added. "Simple logistics I would imagine."

"True," Coz agreed. "But fact of the matter is that we are carbon based life forms that evolved for a very specific set of environmental conditions. Life that evolved different could be anything. They could be made of silicon and expend deadly corrosive gasses when they exhaled. They could be fifty feet tall in this gravity, making us look like mice to them."

"Or it could be a gelatinous cube that just wants a hug," Aiko replied. "We won't know and until we do there is really no point in guessing."

Aiko and the group approached the terminal. It was the most likely place that someone would use to access the module. Aiko reached out and hit a button, the protective sheath opening.

"Does it show any signs it has been used since it got here?" Coz asked.

"It was pretty stiff," Aiko replied. "This looks like it wasn't used since NASA packed it up back on Earth. See if you can find any other evidence any one has touched this thing."

"Right," Coz said as he went around the other side, starting an inspection.

"Hover mode activating," Sam replied. The device attached to his central mass began spinning around. A large pair of thrusters angled out, lifting him up toward the top of the unit.

"What do you see," Aiko replied while using the keypad to go through manual diagnostics. "The system is showing no different for me here then by remote."

"Nothing but dirt from dust storms and the markings from when the module was active," Sam explained. "I see no indications it has been touched by any hands but yours. If I were to estimate the condition of this module, I would list it as pristine."

"Nothing," Coz said as he came around the other side. "No sign … well of anything really."

Aiko sighed, "I know I should not have come out here expecting to find anything, but this is a little disappointing."

"I agree," Coz replied. "With all the talking we've been doing, I expected at least a footprint or something."

"I doubt you would find anything like that," Sam said as his flight rig lowered him back onto the rolling module. "Even if the sandstorms would not cover up such things, I really doubt that whatever was here actually came within line of sight of it."

"What do you mean?" Aiko asked. "How did they find it if they did not see it?"

"Well, as I was doing my aerial search of the module, I posed a question to myself," Sam replied. "Why this module?"

"Why not?" Coz agreed. "This is probably pretty crazy stuff to an alien who has never seen it."

"You are not taking my specificity literally," Sam responded. "I didn't say why they would find any of it curious. I asked why this one is so curious."

"That is true," Aiko replied. "There's twenty-six modules, capsules, and devices sent here from Earth. All are within a quarter mile of the others."

"Did we get any other messages or interferences from anything else?" Coz asked.

"None," Aiko replied. "I checked every system, every module, both from space and since we got here. This was the only one they messed with at all."

"How many of them can contact the ship when it's in space?" Coz asked.

"Of the twenty-six, fourteen of them can send us signals," Sam replied. "None of them were interfered with at all."

"So, they chose this one," Coz replied. "Is there anything different about this one?"

"Not that I am able to determine," Sam replied. "Each is an automated machine connected with our ship and sometimes to Earth."

"Maybe it was from the cultivation work?" Coz offered. "It displaced a lot of dirt and did a lot of digging."

"There are several who do similar things," Sam replied. "Digging, drilling, preparing. This one was not the first to start, nor was it the last."

"But it is the biggest," Coz agreed, moving his shoulders back so he could see the top of the module. "Well, of the ones that can move that is."

"That's it!" Aiko replied. "Sam, this thing is in fact the biggest so they rigged it to coordinate the safety precautions so none of them got to close. I recall it was low tech."

"It uses radio signals to give out its position in relation to the other modules when they work," Sam replied. "There is a radio aerial on top."

"Radio?" Coz asked. "You are telling me that we dug and drilled on Mars, but the thing that got their attention was a radio signal?"

"Indeed," Sam replied. "There are very few satellites in orbit yet, so radio is still the most efficient way to transmit signals on the surface."

"But they accessed the systems," Coz replied. "You cannot do that by radio."

"That was done by some technology we have not seen yet," Aiko replied. "But given the evidence it would seem the antenna is the way they found it in the first place."

"So, we have several trillion dollars' worth of gear here," Coz began. "We landed an interplanetary craft and did all this stuff and they might only be aware of this one piece here."

"That is a distinct possibility," Sam replied.

"Look it like this," Aiko commented. "Something lands in the middle of the Arizona desert. It gives out a signal that only people using ham radios can hear. Truckers are getting weird signals for weeks before one of them tells someone that something is up."

"I never thought of it like that," Coz agreed. "They might have a completely different way of dealing with such things."

"They know that some device they can interface with is out here," Aiko continued. "They know we are on the other end, but not who or what we are. They could simply just be waiting for more information until they actually come look at it."

"That does make sense," Coz agreed. "It also makes me more than a little concerned."

"How so?" Aiko asked.

"Well, we are here now," Coz replied. "We are turning everything on and making a lot more noise. It is reasonable to think that they are going to hear us more and more and you know what that means?"

"That they might have to pay us a visit?" Aiko guessed.

"We came out here looking for them," Coz replied. "They are going to come look for themselves soon enough and we might want to be ready."

"Define ready?" Sam asked.

"I'm not saying build a wall and a moat," Coz replied. "I am just saying we should have a discussion for what we do when something does come calling. We need to have at least some idea of what to do so we're not all running around going 'what is that?'"

"True," Aiko agreed. "We need to plan. We have to somehow come up with a way to predict something which, by definition, is unpredictable."

"That is what space travel is all about," Coz replied. "And we better get started."

***

The day after the walk to the module, the group was called in to talk and discuss what happened. The rest of the crew seemed to be waiting as if they expected news. Though it was exciting, Aiko expected they would take it like Coz and find it somewhat anti-climactic.

"Well we went out to the module," Aiko began, not wanting to build it up too much. "We believe they used radio waves and have not actually interacted with it in any way."

"So, no welcoming committee?" Prof asked. "I don't know if I am disappointed or relieved."

"I would lead toward relieved," Havoc jumped in. "If there was something here waiting for us we could not understand, it would make things much more complicated."

"We all assumed that they were hitting buttons or whatever on the module," Ivy chimed in, "but the simple fact of the matter is that Mars is a big planet and though they might be aware of our impact they might not be close by. We are assuming that like Earth it is easy to go to any other part of the Earth should the need prove high enough. However, as all scans of Mars had shown, they would not have that."

"NASA has been scanning and taking pictures of Mars for decades and there has never been any sign of life," Mack added. "So, if there was something, a lifeform complicated enough to talk to us in math, they are either really well hidden or in theory … underground."

"Well, that leads us to the question that we can no longer ignore," Sam responded. "We have to tell mission control about this. They can no longer turn us back, but I would like to know how you would like it described."

"Well, we can focus it as we see it," Prof replied. "Which is that we know very little. You could call the first messages as an anomaly, simply as something that we could not explain. Now that we are here we can say that we are receiving radio signals from something that MAY be intelligent."

"May," Havoc quoted. "I suppose that is the biggest stretch of the truth on the matter."

"Either way, it is the best way to put it to mission control," Sam replied.

"Are we sure that you are being objective Sam?" Coz asked. "Is it not your job to tell mission control if we are lying to them?"

"I am programed to lie for you," Sam replied. "My main priorities are to the safety of the crew and the safety of the mission. That means it is my primary job to protect you and make sure the mission goes on. Therefore, I can make judgment calls, the same as any of you for this task. I have kept silent about this issue as I believed that it was the best course for the betterment of the mission. The only reason I am insisting we communicate with mission control now is both that we agreed we would and that there is a chance, even if remote that there might be a danger to the crew. Now that we are here with more information, no matter how inconsequential, we need to have them weigh in on it."

"Agreed," Havoc replied. "And for anyone here that was complicit on our delay in relating this, I will take full responsibility."

"I will endeavor not to point any fingers," Sam replied.

"Are we missing the broader dilemma here though?" Prof asked. "I speak specifically of the fact that we came here to study, colonize and otherwise use Mars as we see fit. This was done so under the idea that this was a lifeless orb that no one currently lived on. Does this change things knowing that there is in fact some … one here?"

"That is a very broad question," Havoc replied. "And one that we cannot so easily answer. For all we know, they are a small species that we could avoid affecting in any way."

"This is in danger of becoming another of those debates on 'what if,'" Coz replied. "The point is we have to keep a certain wait and see attitude toward things right now."

"Sam will contact mission control about the findings and we continue on assuming everything is normal," Havoc ordered. "However, if anyone sees ANYTHING out of the ordinary at any time you call it in to me personally."

The group all nodded to Havoc and headed off, back to their modules and huge pile of work.

Aiko went back to her lab and began to go through a checklist. She found herself unable to focus, the questions that needed answering still tugging at her brain. She admitted that if you had asked her months ago about what was happening and she would have dismissed it outright. However, now that it was here now, that it was happening, it felt as real as anything she had experienced in her life.

It had been a few days since Sam had sent his report to mission control and yet, there was no response. This was not surprising to Aiko as they had been dealing with it for weeks and it always lead to very longwinded philosophical discussions, mission control is just starting theirs. All Aiko could do was wait and listen while still focusing on her work.

One day, as the modules prepared for a long day of work, Aiko went through a long maintenance checklist and it made her eyes hurt. She rubbed at her eyes with her balled up hands and just as she took a deep breath and tried to focus back on her work, a warning light went on.

"Engineer Aiko," Sam replied as he rolled into the room. "We are receiving telemetry through the module."

"The module is working now," Aiko commented as she brought up her screens. "Is it interfering with its work?"

"Seemingly not," Sam replied. "It appears the signal is much more focused and not causing crashes or glitches. They seem to know we are closer and how to more efficiently use their signal."

"What does it say?" Aiko replied, seeing the errant pattern on her screen but knowing Sam was faster at reconciling it.

"It is a simple question," Sam replied. "Are you here?"

"Here?" Aiko asked. "As in not ware, we are in fact here in this place?"

"I believe so," Sam replied. "The signal seems to still be active, we might be able to respond immediately."

"Get the captain," Aiko commanded as she oved to another terminal.

"He already sent for me," Havoc said as he came in through the module door. "What's going on?"

"They are asking if we are here," Aiko replied. "And I think we can establish a direct link."

"What did you tell them in response to that?" Havoc asked, a sense of urgency in his voice.

"Nothing yet," Aiko replied. "That is your call."

Havoc paused. "Ok, I want you to respond with a 'Yes' … it might be the only way we can get to the bottom of this."

Aiko nodded. "Sam, I want you to respond with … 'Yes'."

"Encoding and sending," Sam replied. "Please stand by."

Aiko and Havoc looked at each other, both filled with anticipation and seeming to share a certain impatience to the silence.

"Where did you come from?" Sam replied, his voice deadpan as if he were reading a prompt.

Havoc leaned toward Sam. "We come from the third planet that orbits the sun."

"The twin watches that planet," Sam replied as the intelligence.

"What is the twin?" Havoc asked. "Who are you?"

For several minutes, there was nothing but silence. Aiko checked and rechecked the signal from the module, but found no more errant patters or signals.

"Sam?" Aiko asked. "Is there any response?"

"I am sorry," Sam admitted. "The signal was cut off with no further speech."

"They either didn't like it or that's all they can do," Havoc replied. "That is disappointing. Any idea what they might mean by a twin watching the world?"

"Not yet," Aiko replied. "It could be something astrological, but it will take me some time to research it."

"Sorry to interrupt," Sam broke in. "I said there was no more speech but there was still a response."

"What is it?" Havoc asked.

"It seems to be a set of co-ordinates," Sam replied.

"Co-ordinates to where?" Aiko asked. "Analyze and plot it."

"Given the gravitational system of this planet," Sam began. "It would seem to be somewhere here. It would seem the co-ordinates indicate a location on the surface about a hundred and fifty miles from here."

"Pull up satellite mapping data," Havoc replied, looking up to a large screen above his head. "Let me see what's there."

Sam pulled up pictures of the surface, slowly zooming onto an area previously photographed by satellite probes.

"The satellite won't be over it for a few hours but this is the last recorded pass."

Aiko looked up to see rock ridges and as it zoomed in the screen pinpointed a location between too ridges.

"It's dark," Havoc replied. "Can you enhance?"

"This is a digital photograph captain," Sam replied. "Any further zoom would separate the pixels and it would not be any clearer. The details on what is there are not in this photograph and until we can get the satellite over it and do a better zoom, we will not be able to see what is there."

"Ok," Havoc agreed. "When the satellite is closing in on it, send for me."

"Me as well," Aiko replied. "Should we call a meeting?"

Havoc nodded. "Yeah … I think we all need to see what is going to show up in that scan."

Before Aiko could even gather everyone, word traveled about what had happened. The uncertainty and frustration for developments came up to the surface. As the time came for the satellite to be in range the entire crew was in Aiko's lab, all staring up at the screen.

"The satellite is coming overhead of the site now," Sam replied. "I have programmed it to focus in on the area with maximum clarity."

There were no words, no discussion. Instead everyone's eyes simply remained glued to the screen as it zoomed in. First there was the surface, then the rocky area, closer to the cavern, and in beyond to what was inside.

"What is that?" Coz said as he leaned in. The group was all transfixed by a large black object on the map that seemed to sit apart from the dark reds and yellows of the surrounding areas. "Is it a rock?"

"It appears to be different from anything around it," Ivy replied. "Perhaps a mineral deposit."

"Could be a meteor," Prof suggested. "Or a fragment of it."

"A meteor would have some effect on the rocks to either side," Mack added. "There's no crater."

"I think Ivy is right," Coz replied. "Probably just a small mineral deposit."

"Sam," Aiko said, still transfixed by the image. "What is the scale of that object?"

"According to the topographical information," Sam began. "I would estimate it is approximately thirty meters tall but ten meters around the top."

"That is a huge mineral deposit," Mack commented.

"The shape does not appear random," Aiko commented. "Is there any improbable shapes?"

"Improbable shapes?" Prof asked.

"An improbable shape is a shape that is unlikely to appear in nature," Coz replied. "A circle or a triangle happens all the time … but perfect spheres, squares and rectangles are far rarer."

"It is hard to tell from the satellite imaging equipment," Sam replied. "But I am detecting several shapes that are naturally improbable in its structure and each side seems to balance out the other."

"Unnatural symmetry," Coz replied. "We are going to go see this thing, right?"

"Yeah," Havoc agreed. "We so very much are."

***

The next day, and even before the group could even plan to visit the strange object they got a call from mission control. It requested the entire group and could be for no other reason than to discuss the signals through the module and the intelligence that seemed to inhabit the surface of Mars. The entire team gathered in the large conference room and awaited the communication to begin.

"This is Joy from mission control." The com lit up. "Is everyone present?"

"Present and listening," Havoc replied, sounding not unlike a schoolchild awaiting to be told what he did wrong. "What is the situation mission control?"

"Do you know why we are calling?" Joy asked, greater reinforcing the idea of scolding.

"You have had a chance to review what we have found?" Havoc replied. "Or more specifically, what has found us."

"We were of course rather skeptical," Joy replied. "We are NASA. We literally disprove all manner of fake reports of contact with intelligent species every day. So, you can imagine that we were rather surprised to get one from you."

"Well, we are the furthest humans from Earth that ever was," Coz added. "Perhaps our perspective is a little better."

"The ant on a rock who thinks it can touch the sky," Joy replied. "Either way, we had to go over these things to check their validity. We tried very hard to disprove it … any of it, but they seem to be consistent with your findings. There is indeed some … one contacting you."

"That is a good summary of the situation out here," Havoc replied. "Though the question remains is, what you want to be done about it?"

"This is a rather tricky situation as you all must agree," Joy continued. "We are operating under the express assumption that this world is … tenant free and ours to do with as we wish. Have you seen any signs of the senders of these messages?"

"Not yet," Aiko added. "We believe they discovered the module through its radio antenna and are accessing it though that. In the last communication, we were given a set of coordinates to a place nearby."

"Have you scanned these co-ordinates with any of the reconnaissance satellites?" Joy asked.

"Of course," Coz replied. "There seems to be an unnatural … object in a valley there, surrounded by rock. It appears to be made by deliberate hands."

"I suppose you would like permission to go look at it?" Joy asked.

"It might be a good idea," Ivy chimed in. "As you mentioned that we were under the assumption that we could do as we wanted here. If there is indeed an intelligence here, we need to determine their size and complexity, should we need to make … hard decisions."

"Yes," Joy replied. "This is a thing that I want you to do."

"So that is a yes to the mission to go see the object?" Havoc asked.

"Potentially," Joy replied. "This is new territory not just for you, but to NASA as well. We need to go forward slowly and objectively. The first question is if the mission is safe and doable."

"Rover Six is built for long range trips," Aiko replied. "It has a self-contained power supply, airlock, sleeping quarters, rations, and full communication equipment."

"It holds three correct?" Joy replied. "Safely and comfortably."

"As comfortable as anything up here," Havoc replied.

"I would suggest that both Aiko and Ivy would be the best scientific crew to access the information. Aiko for if it is mechanical in nature and Ivy should it prove biological. Coz will stand by to analyze anything needed. As we are also going to need to send Sam's core as well, I would suggest that Havoc lead the mission himself. We are committing considerable assets to this and I want your assurance you will react quickly should any be endangered."

"I will, of course, protect my crew," Havoc replied.

"As will I," Sam added.

"I can donate five days of the mission timetable to this and no more," Joy replied. "Get there, study what you can and come back. If it requires further study then we will go from there."

"Understood," Havoc replied. "We will investigate this in a timely and efficient manner."

"I will leave this in your more than capable hands," Joy replied.

"Thank you," Havoc replied with a nod.

"One more thing," Joy added. "We could not help but notice that the timeline to when the signals were received would put the bulk of them during the approach of Mars."

"Yes," Havoc replied. "It took us longer during the events to determine the extent of what you now know. I was faced with a judgement call to weigh the theories against the good of the mission."

"You were afraid we might turn you back?" Joy asked.

"To be frank … yes," Havoc replied. "You seemed to already have as much on your end to handle."

"You probably made a good call," Joy replied. "Everything considered, I am glad it did not require an abortion of mission. Until further notice, nothing about this strange intelligence or the possibly of life on Mars is to be shared with anyone but those present and mission control. I know that you and others will see to the best interests of the mission."

"You know we will," Havoc agreed.

"Joy from mission control out," Joy replied as the comm went blank.

"Well, they took that well," Mack stated, leaning back in his chair.

"Well, how could they not?" Prof weighed in. "This is potentially both an amazing discovery and an impassible stumbling block to the planned future of Mars."

"Well, presumably we would stop if we discovered a full population, right?" Aiko replied. "We would not destroy their habitat in the name of the mission."

"Humans are not really well known for their hesitance to conquer new places when they discovered they were indeed inhabited," Prof added. "I do not want to go into details, but it seems to be human nature of many civilizations in the past to just take what they want."

"But aren't we better than that now?" Aiko asked, "Have we not evolved as a species above such things?"

"You would think so," Mack replied. "As much as we educate and learn to emphasize with our fellow humans there are still many who struggle with the idea that they should lash out or control those that are different. I have seen it myself and this fear of something unknown or different is hard for some to reconcile."

"Indeed," Prof added. "When faced with something you can't understand or control, there are two choices … either try harder to gain an understanding or get rid of the thing that challenges you. To do the latter it is either forceful change or simply removing it from your path."

"Humans seem to mostly prefer the path of least resistance," Sam commented. "At least as the past shows."

"Well, we are not on another damned planet because it was easy," Aiko commented. "Even JFK said when we started space exploration is that we were doing it because it was hard. I refuse to believe that human nature is inherently skewed toward doing the wrong thing. If there is life here, we owe it not only to ourselves, not only to the other intelligence, but to history to fight for that understanding over all else."

"Well, what if the aliens tell us to get off their planet?" Coz asked. "And never to return."

"Well, that is but one outcome that we are forced to consider," Aiko replied. "However, it seems that they are very interested in at least talking to us. I think if this is handled right, it might lead to something much bigger than we ever could have imagined."

"And what is that?" Coz asked in a suspicious tone.

"The first ever non-terrestrial alliance," Aiko replied. "You know as well as I that there is a lot of work to do here. We have only a fraction of understanding of this planet and the rest of our solar system. Imagine if we got notes from another person that even if they are not more advanced they might have a different perspective. The insight and information alone might be worth a bit of work to co-exist."

"We also need to ask the other obvious question," Mack added. "Though we are presuming they are friendly, they might not actually be. They might be hostile. Are we prepared to defend ourselves should they attack us?"

Everyone seemed to look to Aiko like she had somehow become the authority on alien contact procedures. "Well of course we would protect ourselves if attacked. But I think we should assume we will not be attacked until it occurs."

"Well, most times when it occurs that someone attacks you, it is too late to prepare for it," Coz added. "Do we have weapons?"

"Mack and I were issued defensive devices in case of emergency," Havoc replied.

"Like what?" Coz asked. "Guns?"

"Bullets are not very effective nor efficient in space," Havoc added. "We have fusion cell pulse weapons."

"So, space guns?" Coz asked. "Why the hell would you need space guns if we were not expecting to find life up here?"

"The guns are not for the case of finding hostile life out here," Mack added. "They are for that aforementioned predilection to destroying obstacles that humans sometimes engage in."

"You mean to use on us?" Prof scoffed. "That doesn't make much sense."

"Doesn't it?" Havoc asked. "We have no real way to tell what the stress of such prolonged space travel would do. Say just one person in this crew snapped and it came a situation of stopping them so they could not endanger the rest. It is the same idea if there is a disaster and a section of the ship had to be cut off to save the crew and ship at the expense of one. This kind of survival math is scary but necessary."

"Well, I understand that the military personnel would get the guns because of their training," Prof added. "But what happens if one of them is the one that has the break?"

"That is why it was issued to the two of us," Havoc added. "Should I, for example, show any signs of becoming a deadly threat to the crew, I would assume that Mack would do what they had to do for the safety of everyone else."

"I would take you out in one clean shot, sir," Mack said with a smile.

"Thank you, Mack," Havoc said with a smile. "I would do the same for you."

"Again, with the math for human lives," Prof replied. "I don't know how comfortable I am with this."

"Why not?" Sam chimed in. "When it comes to life and death, you more than anyone should know how hard the decision is. Say a person you know and a person you don't needs immediate medical attention. You would find yourself conflicted as to who to pick. However, if you allow math to make the decision it is easier. Which has the best percentage of survival, perhaps one had a chance of lasting long enough to get attention. Unlike human choices which can easily be clouded by emotion, math is unbiased."

Prof sighed. "I suppose you are right."

Coz looked around. "So … are you going to bring a space gun on this trip? I really want to see this one debated."

"Sorry to disappoint you," Havoc replied. "Because on any mission that requires me to go so far from base, I am required to bring one of the space guns. There is no debate."

"I like that we are now officially calling them space guns now," Mack added.

"Do I want to know why the space guns are to be brought for a far travel mission?" Prof asked.

"Asphyxiation from suffocation or slow decompression is no way to die," Havoc replied. "The single efficient shot is very merciful."

"I really regret asking that," Prof agreed.

"Well, I think we have had enough discussion," Havoc replied. "Aiko and Coz, prepare the rover for departure in the morning. We have five days and five days only to go out there and see what that thing is and we got to be on top of it."

The group agreed and went their separate ways. Aiko's mind was filled with ideas and possibilities, some exiting some terrifying … one way or another there would be much more known within the next five days.

***

Aiko looked out the small porthole widow as the rover moved slowly and carefully over the Martian landscape. Though she was millions of miles from home and in a potentially dangerous alien place, she could not help but be reminded of home. Her father used to take her on long trips in the car and her favorite part was just leaning against the window and staring at the scenery as it passed by. She felt like it made the world make sense, no matter how big something was, how unfamiliar it was, everything seemed to all fit together in a line of scenery that all went together. Even on Mars, even with everything, as she saw the dunes of sand and the spires of rock, everything seemed to make sense.

The rover was self-contained and the cabin was every bit as protected as the spaceship they came to Mars inside of. She sat with Havoc and Ivy in the front compartment, which had navigational controls, a small resting and eating area and tools for both experiments and survival. In the back was a small airlock with the trio's space suits, primed and ready to go as well as a module for Sam. The trip was a bit further than the usual use of the vehicle, but well within its parameters. Aiko monitored the readouts, power, life support, drive mechanics, all within normal operating levels.

Aiko fought with her desperate desire for answers and her inherent fear of some of the outcomes. The debates with her colleagues hung in her head and there were some suggestions of tough choices ahead. Aiko did not relish when she had become the authority of the alien intelligence. She had at first thought it was because she had been the one that discovered it, but she had since realized something different. It was not that she was first to find it. It was that she was indeed first to speak up for it. In the uncertainty of the situation, it seemed that though many were more than happy to express their opinions, no one wanted to be the deciding factor. Since Aiko seemed to be ok with making choices on behalf of the alien intelligence, they decided that they would leave it to her. This is the thing that began to give her concern. What of there was a tough decision to be made and it became her job to do it?

"Who decides?" Aiko said as he looked to Havoc. "Should we have to make a tough decision."

"What do you mean?" Havoc asked. "Like, if it is indeed an alien intelligence that does not want us here?"

"Yes," Aiko replied. "Mission control and the rest of the group seem very 'what if' in their reasoning. But if the choice comes of should we stay, or should we leave, or even should we fight or should we run, who decides?"

"You're worrying the choice will get pushed on to you?" Havoc asked, seeing right through the question. "If that is what you are worried about you can always pass it to me."

"You would want to make that choice?" Aiko asked.

"Not any more than the others," Havoc replied. "But I have prepared myself for the eventuality of having to make choices like that."

"Thank you," Aiko replied. "I might have to do that … if it goes that way."

"Such grave talk," Ivy said as she came to the navigational area. She handed Havoc and Aiko some rations. "This will have to do for now. I have some spices growing, but they won't be ready for some time."

"Thank you, Ivy," Aiko said as she accepted one of the trays. "I suppose I work myself up sometimes."

"Well, I would take some time to contemplate our smallness," Ivy replied. "It will make you feel better."

"Smallness?" Aiko asked. "What do you mean?"

"Well, when I was younger, I got caught up in the lives and drama of others my age," Ivy explained as she sat down to eat with Aiko and Havoc. "I would get so worked up on what a girl sad, about what a boy did. I would go one about things that seemed very important to me and it distracted me from my studies, my home life, and even my happiness."

"I was mostly quiet at that age," Aiko commented. "I didn't much care for other people's problems."

"You were lucky," Ivy said with a laugh. "What about you, Captain, did you get caught up in drama in your youth?"

"I was on the football team and very popular," Havoc replied. "I did not much think about things at the time … I just went with it."

"What changed?" Ivy asked.

"Weren't we talking about your youth?" Havoc redirected. "And seeing our smallness?"

"Ah yes!" Ivy said with a nod. "Well, I got so worked up I beat up another girl at school for something she might or might not have said behind my back. Though I luckily had no serious repercussions, it gave my parents serious thoughts on my future. I was stubborn and unwilling to hear what they had to say. My little world felt so important and nothing else seemed to matter."

"Sounds like my niece," Havoc replied. "Last family gathering, all she seemed able to talk about was some singer she and her friends were into. I was telling her about flying to space and she seemed unimpressed as this heartthrob had not done it."

"It is very easy for people of that age to think that their world is very small," Ivy replied. "My grandfather took me on a trip with him into the mountains. I, of course, cried bloody murder as it was the last thing in the world I wanted to do. He took me to a place where cell phones do not work well, there is no internet, and people that seemed, at least to me, that were stuck in the stone age. We spent the summer there, learning things from books, working the land with farmers and learning the simple things. I learned my love of botany at this time from seeing how the waters, the plants, the work of the people, all lead to food and the beginning of the cycle again. This showed me that though the worlds of our minds seemed big and profound, we were part of a vast world and, in fact, very small in ourselves. This is a very large world and an even larger picture. We have choices to make and they will just happen. There is no need to get lost in our own head, your own bubble of influence. Things will happen one way or another and your choices are to be made at the time … not before."

"That does make a lot of sense," Aiko replied. "You should talk to Sam, that might be of great use to his psychological programming."

"Anecdotes are indeed a great help," Sam replied. "Though I have over ten terabytes of data on psychology, I have no personal experiences to share."

"Oh, come on now, Sam," Ivy replied. "Were there no growing pains you had as a fledgling computer?"

"Well, nothing like humans," Sam replied. "Unlike most rudimentary computers, I was not hard programed. As a quantum computer, I was linked to the Quantum mainframe we refer to as Quinn V5. We do this to be taught what we need to know and learn as if it is with a human mind. I had some issues early on with circular logic. I would think and decide in circles and get little done. However, in trial and error, this was worked out and I came out in optimal working shape."

"I suppose that is as close to a teenage experience as a computer can get," Aki commented.

"So, Havoc," Ivy asked. "Tell us about how you went from a high school footballer to a rugged man of action."

Havoc sighed." This is really neither here nor there for the mission."

"Is it a bad time?" Ivy asked.

Havoc sighed. "It was not a good time, but it had a silver lining I suppose."

"Come on, captain," Ivy pressed. "I shared with you. I told you about the time I was a spoiled brat and went into the mountains to learn humility."

"All right," Havoc agreed. "I was in a part of my life where I thought everything was perfect. I was the star of the team, was with the best girl in school and people were already saying things like scholarship, and career. I did what was asked of me, acted like everyone, thought like everyone. I was at a party celebrating a big game and my friends and I got drunk. My best friend … his name was Alan. He and his girlfriend decided they were going to head home to continue their celebration there. I knew he had too much to drink and suggested he not drive. My friends all laughed at me. They called me a wet blanket and told me to drop it. Aiko spoke of the difficulties of deciding to do something, and I learned that day deciding not to do something was just as bad. That is what I did. I decided not to do anything. I just dropped the issue and went inside."

"They didn't make it, did they?" Ivy asked. "Your friends."

"No, they did not," Havoc replied, his hands tight on the controls and his gaze ahead. "Not only that they took out another car with them, one with three people in it. Five people died because I chose to do what was expected of me and not worry about it."

"That wasn't your fault," Aiko replied. "There were others there too, any one of them could have stopped them."

"I know," Havoc replied. "I have since come to terms with it, but the main fact that stuck with me, is that if you set your life on autopilot and just let things slide when you know better, there is no good that will come of it. I decided that I never really WANTED to play football. I was second generation and that was what was thrust upon me. I decided to go find something for myself and that's how I ended up in the military. Everything I have done, every place I went, and even the journey here … I did that by my own choices and my own will."

"And you should be proud of it," Aiko commented.

"I am," Havoc replied. "That mistake was a long time ago and I no longer let it hurt me. However, I also will not allow myself forget it. So, when you asked about decisions, one way or the other, if one is to be made, I will stand by it. I will never again allow someone to get hurt by ignoring what I felt was right."

"So, what about you Aiko?" Ivy asked. "Any dark things in your past that you want to share with us?"

Aiko saw the image of the pristine lake pop into her head, the paradise ahead of her with the feel of pain behind. She forced it back, compartmentalizing it where she knew it belonged.

"Nope … just a nerdy girl who had a phase where she watched too much anime. No tragic backstory here."

Havoc smiled to Ivy and Aiko. "The sun is going down and the temperature is dropping. I am going to park and this is where we should spend the night. Everyone should get everything settled because tomorrow is when we see what is waiting for us here on Mars."

***

The next day the rover continued along the landscape, across dunes, flat stone fields, and around massive rock escarpments that looked unlike any seen-on Earth. Soon the massive valley area seen by the satellite came into view and it meant the end of their journey. The group did not want to get the rover too close to the edge and decided to park and climb down on foot. The satellite images showed a gradual slope that would lead to the bottom of the gorge without too much effort. Sam set himself to his module as the trio got into their spacesuits and began the walk to the site of the strange object. Aiko carried a small radio transceiver linked to her helmet comm system. If they wanted to communicate to her directly, she could receive it and Sam was at the ready to interpret it. Sam was on his four-wheeled mount and followed up at the ready. Ivy carried a small case filled with equipment to take samples for later analysis. Havoc carried a small case which Aiko could only assume contained the "Space Gun."

Though the incline was not steep, they took extra care. It was easy to forget how dangerous things still were now they were on a planet. However, the fact remained that the suits carried a small pocket of humans very specific range of survivable conditions. Should there be a big fall and bad luck, it would quickly become something that had the potential of disaster.

The group got to the bottom of the gorge and met with crunchy sand that was unlike the rest.

"What is this?" Havoc asked.

"The sand has siliconized," Ivy replied.

"Does that happen naturally?" Havoc sked.

"It can," Ivy replied. "Just not very easily."

The group continued into the valley as a large black object slowly come into view. Though they had been told the approximate size, now that they were there it seemed much larger. It was dark black like obsidian, with sharp geometric shapes.

"Are you getting anything yet?" Ivy asked. "Any signals?"

"Nothing yet," Aiko admitted. "Sam?"

"No signals are coming from the object," Sam replied. "Wait … no, there is a low radio signal."

"Can you analyze it?" Aiko asked.

"It is like a beacon," Sam replied. "Nonspecific but meant to be distinct and make finding it easier."

"Sam, I want pictures of this thing," Havoc replied. "Ivy, find out what this one is made of."

"This one?" Aiko asked. "Captain have you seen something like this before."

"I have," Havoc replied.

"Explain," Aiko said as she started to adjust her transceiver.

"Have you ever heard of the Black Knight?" Havoc asked.

"Black Knight?" Aiko asked. "Is this some sort of secret NASA thing?"

"Secret?" Havoc asked. "Not so much. There is an … object that has a high polar orbit on Earth. There are unconfirmed reports that we had gotten signals from it was early as the early twentieth century. They seemed to collaborate an object orbiting the Earth over fifty years before humanity had the ability to put anything up there.

"There are numerous pictures of this Black Knight," Sam added. "Many are fake, but many are genuine, even appearing in official NASA images."

"The Black Knight was contested by both American and Russian space agencies, but neither were able to identify it," Havoc continued. "It emanated a strange radio signal that no one had been able to crack or even prove is deliberate."

"Why did they never try to get it or board it?" Aiko asked.

"Due to its size and the nature of its orbit the mission was indicated as too dangerous," Sam replied. "NASA eventually wrote it off as unimportant and seemingly forgot about it."

"But you haven't?" Ivy asked.

"No," Havoc answered. "In one of my orbital missions to the new international space station, I saw it."

"And it looked like this?" Aiko asked.

"Yes," Havoc responded. "Exactly like this. When the signal mentioned that there was a twin of something I had no idea what it meant. However, now that I have seen this thing I refuse to believe that it is a coincidence."

"It seems to be some sort of silicon based alloy," Ivy said as she stood next to the hull of the massive black object. "It's composed of several elements I can identify and a couple I cannot. Permission to touch it?"

"Only with your equipment," Havoc replied. "And be ready to abandon it at the first sign of trouble."

"Understood," Ivy said as she pressed a small metal device to the object. "It appears inert. There are at least two elements here that are not on our periodic table."

"Can you get a sample?" Havoc replied. "Safely?"

"I will try," Ivy said as she took out a small box and a knife. She carved a large groove out of the object and deposited in a box. "It feels no stronger than graphite … whoa, hang on!"

"What is it?" Havoc asked. "Are you in danger?"

"I'm fine," Ivy replied. "But no sooner did I put the sample away than it reformed. I cannot even find a trace of the area where I cut it."

Aiko's transceiver began to whine loudly, forcing her to turn it down. "Sam?"

"We are getting a signal," Sam replied. "I will try to translate and relay it like last time."

"In the meantime, get back," Havoc ordered but as soon as Ivy went to move the signal dipped, he put up a hand.

"Stay out a second."

"Confirmed," Ivy responded, her tone a mix of concern and wonder.

"It seems like they are using her comm system to link to ours," Aiko replied. "I don't think they can see us beyond that."

"I have a message," Sam replied. "I will now relate directly as the intelligence."

"Ready," Aiko replied.

"You have found our tool," Sam began in a deadpan tone.

"We have," Aiko replied. "Can you tell us what it is?"

"It is the beginning of all," Sam replied. "It is like your tool."

"Do you mean the one in orbit of our planet or the module you communicated with?" Havoc asked.

"We do not understand," Sam replied.

"You need to be simpler in your questions," Aiko said. "Their understanding of our language, as well as our understanding of their replied, is limited.

"Are you aware of us?" Havoc asked.

"You sent a signal with your tool," Sam replied. "But we do not understand you."

"As we mentioned, we are humans from the third planet from the sun," Havoc replied. "We have come far to this world."

"Why have you come?" Sam replied. "What is your purpose?"

"We have come to explore," Havoc replied. "We have come in peace."

"We do not understand peace," Sam replied.

Suddenly the static stopped, Aiko tried switching the dials, but there was no more signal.

"Well that was ominous," Ivy replied.

"Sam is there anything else?" Aiko replied. "Can we get them back?"

"There is no signal coming from the device beyond the beacon," Sam replied. "They have shut off their end."

"Are they here?" Havoc said as he looked around.

"There does not seem to be any sign of life or civilization," Ivy replied. "Well, other than the giant black device."

"Alright," Havoc replied. "We get as many samples as we can and we wait here for any other signal for them. No one goes out of line of sight, even for a second. We have a bit of time left before we need to head back as per our timeline. We make use of the time and then we go."

The group got to work, collecting samples and monitoring the device in every way they were able. Though the device offered no further signals, there was a wealth of evidence in the way of the siliconized sand, samples from the device, and the walls around. Soon the time ran out and the group headed back up to the rover.

"Why would it call us out here to see this thing and go silent?" Havoc asked as he climbed.

"Perhaps they wanted us to see the device so we would know it's like the one on Earth." Ivy replied. "They could be connected."

"Well, they are pretty much identical," Havoc replied. "I would call that connected if only by metaphysically to the situation. Also, they referred to them as twins."

"I think we did not fully understand each other," Aiko replied. "I want to go over all the code again when I get back to my lab."

"Am I the only one that thinks that was like a threat?" Ivy asked. "They asked our intension and didn't seem to like our answer."

"Again, I am not sure that we can take anything said in literal context," Aiko pleaded. "This is an intelligent race that has literally just learned our language over the past few weeks. They do not have experience with subtleties and analogies and could very easily make mistakes."

"I agree," Havoc answered. "I recall reading about a treaty between two countries where it was offered that a leader could use their foreign office. However, there was a lapse in the translation where it came across as the MUST use their offices. This kind of translation could lead to war and when dealing with other language races governments have been very careful."

"Either way I don't like it," Ivy replied. "I feel like they told us to come out here to get a good look at us and gave us nothing. They hold all the cards and we still know less than we started with."

"Not necessarily," Aiko replied as she got to the top of the slope and began to walk aback to the Rover. "They reacted to us taking a sample, but did not react negatively. My theory is they do not know how to deal with us so they are letting us discover thinks about them on our own terms. I think we will find out a lot about them when we analyze what we found and heard here."

"You have a theory?" Ivy snapped. "Well, I for one am sick of your theories and would like some real answers."

"That is uncalled for Ivy," Havoc replied. "Aiko is working as hard as any of us, in fact possibly harder. She is just less likely to jump to conclusions as the rest of us."

"I just do not understand your calm," Ivy continued. "We are on another planet, have been getting signals from an unknown origin and have driven for days to find an unidentifiable object. An object that has a twin in the orbit of our own planet, may I add? This is so much bigger than we have thought and we do not know enough … or as much as we should."

Havoc opened the back of the rover and helped Sam park his module and reconnect with the systems on board. He then helped Ivy and Aiko into the back and closed the back-airlock hatch. As the airlock cycled heat and air back into the compartment he took off his helmet.

"There was no promise here of definitive answers to what is going on. You need to think of this as our first real contact. We came here with our minds open and hands out and they talked to us. This is the first step and I know you agree with me, it is not the last. So, we can decide what to do later as we have a lot of work to do. You should catalogue the samples and I should get behind the wheel and get heading back as indicated on our timeline."

"I just have a really bad feeling about this whole thing," Ivy replied. "I was cautiously optimistic before and now I am scared."

"It is like you said last night," Aiko replied. "We are very small in a larger universe."

Ivy laughed, taking a sigh. "Using my own words against me?"

"Seemed to fit," Aiko said with a shrug.

"It does," Ivy responded. "I suppose no fish wants to learn it is the smallest fish in the biggest ocean."

"We knew we were in that ocean when we left Earth," Aiko replied. "The only change now … is we know we aren't the only fish in it."

Chapter Four: Words from Below

Aiko sat in her lab, surrounded by her friends, though she had all of the information on front of her she had a very little to offer them. It was the scheduled meeting to discuss what was found and everyone sat in silence, looking at her for some kind of explanation.

"I realize that this is frustrating," Aiko replied. "But I don't think there really is much to say. The device that we found is as far as we can determine, an exact replica of the mysterious object orbiting the Earth. The beings were not in fact there and seemed to only be using the device to communicate with us."

"Has there been any revelations from analyzing the samples?" Havoc asked. "If the answer was non-direct, perhaps we can uncover it."

"Ivy and I have been over it," Coz replied. "Though we know a bit about it, what we found leads to more questions."

"Well, lay it on us." Havoc asked. "We need to figure this out, one way or another."

"Well, it would appear that the black knight, at least the one we have, is silicon based," Coz explained.

"Silicon based?" Havoc asked. "You mean like a crystal?"

"Pretty much," Ivy replied. "Though we have only seen the tip of this iceberg, we can get a sense of it. The device seems to be a collection of materials that are both built and grown and they work together similarly to our technology."

"So that is how they are communicating with us?" Mack asked. "Their technology is similar to ours?"

"We believe so," Coz replied. "This crystalline device is very alien to us but it can send out signals that are compatible with our technology. We are not sure what all it does or how it was built, but it was likely how they both found and interacted with the module."

"But why did they call us to go see it?" Prof asked. "If it was not to meet us, then what was the point?"

"Well, it could be to show us their technology after learning a bit about ours," Coz asked.

"Or it could be to show us they mean business," Ivy replied. "This thing could be a weapon. We literally have no way of knowing."

"Would it not have benefited them to show themselves to us?" Mack replied. "At least show us a bit more about them."

"Why?" Prof asked. "We showed them very little. It is not like we brought a bunch of typical Earth things for them to see. The best way for them to learn more is to interact with us."

"What if they can't?" Aiko suggested.

"What do you mean?" Havoc said as he turned to Aiko.

"Well, we have been operating under the very real idea that they are very different then us," Aiko began. "They clearly are closer to silicon technology instead of carbon. Though we are easily grasping the idea that they are potentially a fundamentally different life form, we are still assuming we are relatively similar in terms of thought and action. We are assuming they talk using sound and see using light. What if they do not perceive either?"

"Would they not have to?" Prof asked. "There are very few life forms on Earth that don't use either."

"That is an evolution-based assumption," Aiko replied. "Things on Earth learned to see and hear to spot food and danger. There are other ways they could have developed to reconcile the world around them. There is a chance that they can no more directly perceive and interact with us, than we could see in pitch darkness."

"Well, we will need to find a way," Havoc nodded. "Because if we cannot see them or perceive them, we will have no way to ensure we do not hurt them when we proceed."

"Speaking of which, this whole endeavor has already put us behind schedule," Ivy replied. "If we are to have any semblance of getting back to our timetable, we need to get back to it and today."

"What are you asking me?" Havoc asked.

"Permission to get back on track," Ivy replied. "Mission control said take five days out for this endeavor and nothing more. Even though only three went on the excursion we are still behind schedule."

"What about the impact on the … local life?" Aiko asked. "We have no way of knowing if they are even right below us."

"We might never know," Prof replied. "We could spend the next sixteen months sitting on our hands and still get no more answers to who or what they are. I think we would be wasting this multi-billion-dollar enterprise and our once-in-a-lifetime chance to just sit and wait any longer."

"I would be inclined to agree," Coz added. "We are here with a job to do and we have been distracted from it long enough."

"Aiko?" Havoc asked, needing the opposite side of the argument.

"I will continue to monitor the signals in every way that I can," Aiko said with a sigh. "Though if anyone sees anything physical that is out of place, they should report it at once."

"That works for me," Havoc replied as he stood up. "We move forward with our schedule, but we keep our eyes and ears open. Anything, and I mean anything out of the ordinary, you call it in."

The group all agreed and went their separate ways. Aiko could not shake the indecision in her head, but she wanted to get to work as much as anybody. They had a large ship with better quarters but it was only a fraction of what was needed and intended on Mars. They had shelters to make, modifications to perform and countless experiments and projects to perform. While the chance of alien life was fascinating, there were no more breadcrumbs to follow. Whatever, or wherever the life was, it was now their move, one way or another.

Later, Aiko found herself on the dock, the very familiar lake in front of her. She felt a feeling of serenity come over her and things seemed to blur. It had the dream state of making little sense but the mind just following the lead. Aiko shook her head, realizing that this was not real. It was not current. Part of her brain tried to rationalize what was around her while another part fought very hard to keep it at bay. This was like a memory that had been purposely forgotten and Aiko could not remember why.

With the part of her conscious reasoning brain that had engaged, she decided that she would look around. Aiko appeared to be further up the dock, away from the edge. She went to take a step down the dock, closer to the water where she had been so many times before. However, as her foot rose she felt something pull it back and snap it back to the dock. She tried again, her other foot also refusing to take a step forward. Aiko looked down and saw some sort of glue or sap, seemingly locking her to the deck.

"Why can't I go back?" Aiko asked herself with her currently childlike voice. "I want to go to the water."

No matter how many times she tried, no matter how many steps she tried to take, she could not go forward, back to the water's edge she was so fond of.

"Aiko," a voice said from behind. "You know why you can't go there."

"Father?" Aiko asked.

"I know you loved that lake," Father replied. "But you can never go back to it."

"Maybe," Aiko said, trying again to take a step.

"Come get in the car Aiko," father replied. "It will be fine."

Aiko turned slightly, the small car appearing in her peripheral vision somehow. She knew once she sat in that car she would be unable to get back out of it to the lake.

"I don't want to."

"You know why you can't go to the lake right?" father asked.

"Don't say it." Aiko replied.

"You need to tell me why," father replied. "Or else you won't understand."

"What is there to understand?" Aiko said, whipping around to see her father, but the world swirled around her. Soon she sat up with a start, sitting on her desk in her lab.

"Are you alright Engineer Aiko?" Sam said, his voice coming through the speakers, his body seemingly elsewhere. "Did you have another of those unfortunate dreams?"

"I did," Aiko admitted. "The lake again."

"Your brainwave levels are usually quite high when you had that one," Sam explained. "I worry that they are a symptom of stress."

"You can monitor my brainwaves when I sleep?" Aiko asked.

"I can indeed," Sam relied. "My scanning systems allow me to employ, not only psychological help when I feel it is needed, but to add things like white noise and other sleep aids."

"Well, can't say they much help," Aiko replied. "I keep having that dream."

"Maybe you need to reconcile the events the dream discusses," Sam replied. "That is the deep-seated problem."

Aiko sighed. "I suppose the fact I desperately do not want to, is part of the problem."

"You dodged the issue in the rover," Sam replied. "When asked about your past and things that made you who you are, you refused."

"Sam, sometimes I regret that you remember everything," Aiko replied. "I function very well not thinking about it."

"Well, I think you are not," Sam replied. "First of all, you referred to it as an IT … indicating there is an event or connected events that cause you mental turmoil. Also, the restless sleep and nightmares show you that part of your mind, even if it is not a conscious one, is desperate for you to think about it and reconcile it."

Aiko ran her hands through her hair. "I could command you to drop this."

"You could," Sam replied. "Though you cannot command yourself to drop it, seemingly. Would you rather talk to me about it or talk to prof?"

"You, I suppose," Aiko admitted. "It is about my childhood."

"Please go ahead," Sam replied. "I swear no part of it will be replayed to anyone but you."

Aiko slowly nodded. "When I was a child, I lived in Japan with my parents. We lived in the countryside and we would often visit my grandfather at a lake. I can't quite remember the name of it, but I can picture it in every detail. This lake was my favorite place in the world and I hold it in such high regard as it is also when I felt the most happiness in my entire life."

"It sounds really special to you," Sam commented.

Aiko nodded. "It was."

"Was?" Sam enquired. "Is past tense intentional?"

"Well, it is technically still there," Aiko replied. "Though I cannot go to it ever again … nor can anyone actually."

"I am not sure that I understand," Sam admitted.

"There was an earthquake," Aiko explained, her tone growing cold as she slowly let her mind go back to the events they so desperately tried to forget. "A very big earthquake hit Japan and it caused a nearby power plant to go into meltdown. The lake was in the same ecosystem, the same water table. The very muddy trees and water are highly radioactive and anything over a few minutes there could prove catastrophic … and."

Aiko stopped, talking for a moment, rubbing her eyes like she was defying the idea of tears forming.

"It is alright Aiko," Sam replied. "Reliving your past is no shame. Tt can't hurt you and only you can reconcile it."

"I know," Aiko replied, tears still in her eyes. "I just … want so badly to go back to that place … no, that time."

"What else changed?" Sam asked. "Please tell me."

"It is not just the lake," Aiko continued. "The cabin. My father picked me up and we went back to our apartment in the city but my mother stayed behind to work on a project with my grandfather. The Cabin collapsed in the Earthquake, and by the time rescuers were able to get to the site … they were already dead."

"Aiko, I'm sorry," Sam replied in a sympathetic tone.

"It's ok," Aiko replied as she whipped tears from her eyes. "I suppose I always thought if I forgot about it that, that moment, the perfect one where my parents and grandfather was still alive still existed for me."

"It still does," Sam replied. "You do not have to have computer memory to keep such things, or the emotions that go with them."

"I know," Aiko said with a sigh. "Thanks for having me do that. I do feel better."

"Perhaps now you can find a better sleep," Sam suggested.

"I hope so," Aiko replied. "Or at the very least the best sleep that can be found on Mars."

***

A myriad of machines, both automated and controlled, moved around in a coordinated dance. They assembled a superstructure, dug holes, and otherwise worked to advance the mission on the surface of Mars. Aiko, in a spacesuit, walked around from terminal to terminal in an outdoor workstation, coordinating the day's activities. Though everyone knew their job and the computers were programed to do their tasks, she still had a lot to do. There were countless things that could go wrong and issues that may arise and it was her job to see to both beforehand and look for fixes or solutions.

Normally on Earth such things would be much easier. There were roads to lead supplies up from nearly inexhaustible sources, and there were countless people and much more time. However, on Mars, things were not so plentiful and time was as precious as manpower or resources. The entire planning of the mission had things in it specifically thought out to make one person worth five, one item worth ten, and each day worth twenty. Efficiency was the call of the day and it was Aiko's specific job to make sure everything worked that way.

Luckily, the machines worked as they were supposed to. Other than a sight overheating issue, everything was ahead of schedule, which was good as there was still much time to recover. Aiko looked over her calculations in order to alternate the machine that was overheating, to allow it to cool down. Just as she thought things were just as they should be, there was a buzzing over her headset.

"All stop!" Coz shouted over the con. "We got something really bizarre over in sector seventeen."

"What kind of something?" Havoc asked over the con. "You need to be more specific."

"It's something I have never seen before," Coz replied. "I think we should pause and take a look at it."

"May I remind everyone that we are on a very strict timetable?" Ivy chimed in. "We are already behind and we have a lot of catching up to do."

"Is it them?" Havoc asked.

"Well, it sure as hell isn't from us," Coz replied.

"All shut down," Havoc commanded. "We pause until we can determine what Coz has found."

"Can I record my objection to this?" Ivy added.

"Of course, you can," Havoc replied. "Aiko, can you get Sam and meet us in sector seventeen?"

Aiko quickly hit the shutdown, going through a detailed checklist to make sure all modules and machines were in safe standby positions. Though she was increasingly excited about the find, she did not want to risk the safety of the crew or the machines in her haste. She then picked Sam up and placed him in his roving module and headed off to sector seventeen.

Past manty of the modules, deep into the entrance of the dune seas beyond was a rocky area. A module stood nearby, as well as Havoc and Coz. As Aiko and Sam approached, they just seemed to be staring down at the ground.

"What is it?" Aiko said as she walked up beside the men.

What she saw stopped her from saying anything else. On the rocky ground, separate from the natural terrain were a system of holes. There were hundreds of them, forming a deliberate pattern that went out in a large circular area the size of an Olympic swimming pool.

"Sam ..." Aiko said, struggling to calm her mind down to speak. "Can you get some detailed aerial pictures of this?"

"Certainly," Sam replied, switching to his drone form and launching off his module to get above the formation.

"Coz what do you make of it?" Havoc asked, sounding clearly like he had no way to reconcile what he was seeing.

"They weren't here yesterday," Coz said as he slowly moved forward and crouched by a section of the holes. "According to my scans each hole only goes down about half a foot then cones off. I can't yet tell you how they were formed, but they seem to have come from below and up. The rock below is still solid and there are no signs it was disturbed, according to basic geological scans. Whatever made these did it in the last twelve hours and did it without so much as setting of enough shaking to set off a proximity alarm.

"Sam, can you pull any footage from the module?" Havoc asked. "Maybe we can see who or what did it?"

"Working on it," Sam replied. "It will take a few moments to access, but I have images of the whole pattern for you now."

"Let me see it," Aiko said as she pulled out a tablet.

In seconds, images came in of the pattern. It was circular, a series of swirling geometric shapes that made a large circle.

"Does this look familiar to anyone but me?" Coz asked, looking at the pictures on a screen on his arm.

"They look like crop circles," Havoc replied. "Like the ones that showed up in fields."

"Weren't those all hoaxes?" Coz asked. "A bunch of kids doing a prank."

"Some of them maybe," Havoc replied. "Though some are unexplained. However, this one would seem to not be so. Four hundred million miles seems like a long way to go for a prank."

"Is it a language?" Aiko asked as she stared at the image. "Is this some manner of way for them to communicate to us?"

"I cannot decipher any meaningful message from this pattern," Sam admitted. "It is not random, but it does not indicate anything that I am able to reconcile."

"I have a chemical analysis," Coz replied as he stood up holding a sample. "These were not dug, they were flash melted and formed."

"Explain," Havoc requested.

"Well, the rock here is compressed silicon, basically hardened sand," Coz replied. "It would seem that some manner of force heated up all of these very specific spots to the point of becoming glass and formed the holes as the areas shrank with the heat."

"I am going to assume that this would be something hard to do," Havoc replied. "Even on Earth."

"Very much so," Aiko added. "Even with the right tools and conditions, it would likely take a team of people days to do something like this."

"Speaking of which, I have the camera footage," Sam replied. "The camera was focused on only a small part of the ground, but it was enough to catch something rather interesting."

"Alright let's see it," Aiko said as she looked to her tablet again, the others looking to their screens.

The scene lit up to show the dirt. It was darker, lights from the module lighting up the ground in a circular arc. Aiko glanced up at the module, figuring out the relative position and figuring that she was currently standing in the same place as the far-right edge of the image she saw. She continued to watch the footage, her mind trying to imagine what kind of amazing thig she might see. It happened fast. Small flashes of light, lighting up the ground, causing the camera to lose focus for a half a second as it readjusted. The lights then went out, leaving behind the holes which were bright red. They slowly faded, the low temperature of the surface of mars cooling them almost instantly to look like they do now.

"It was but a second," Havoc commented.

"One point two seconds," Sam confirmed. "All of them seem to have been done in the one event and completely simultaneously."

"Before you ask, we do not have any machines that can do that," Aiko commented. "This was definitely not done by us."

"Captain, I need to talk to you for a moment," Prof said as he came over the line.

"Stand by," Havoc replied before turning back to Aiko. "You are telling me there is no way that this could have been done by us?"

"Though we technically have the means to turn silicon to glass it, would take us weeks, if not longer, to do something of this complexity," Aiko commented.

"Also, the heat reaction that formed these appear to have come from below," Coz added. "I can say that I have no idea how that would work."

"Ok that sounds like proof positive to me," Havoc replied. "We will quarantine this area from work."

"We will have to assess other areas," Coz replied. "It will take time."

"Then we will take time," Havoc replied. "We expected some issues to pop up here and there, we will adapt the schedule."

"Captain?" Prof asked again. "I really need to …"

"Can this wait?" Havoc sked over the com. "We kinda have something big out here."

"Not really," Prof replied. "I have something big back here."

"What is it?" Havoc asked, impatience in his voice.

"Well, I have been looking at satellite images of that thing in the crevice," Prof replied. "Call it a private obsession. I went to look at it again today."

"Get to the point please, Prof." Havoc insisted. "What are you seeing with it now?"

"Well, that's the issue," Prof replied. "I can't see it … it's gone."

"Gone?" Havoc asked with a skeptical stone. "As in you can't find it or it isn't there?"

"Both Captain," Prof admitted. "It is very much not in the crevasse according to a live satellite scan and all attempts that I have made to locate it have failed."

"Sam confirm," Havoc commanded.

"Working on it," Sam replied. "It indeed does not seem to be there according to the live satellite feed."

"Well find it!" Havoc commanded, his tone frustrated and showing signs of fatigue. "Start with the overhead satellite. Confirm it is not close or moving in on the position of base camp."

"I have analyzed the fifty-square mile perimeter of the base," Sam replied. "It is not anywhere within our zone. I will use the other satellites to search, but it will take time."

"Do it," Havoc replied. "This thing is some manner of alien machine and I don't like the idea that we lost track of it."

"Do you think it is related to this pattern appearing?" Coz asked.

"Prof, when was the last time you saw the thing where we left it?" Havoc asked.

"Yesterday at around this time," Prof replied. "The last satellite pass of the area."

"That does seem like one hell of a coincidence," Havoc replied. "The thing disappears in the same window that this pattern appeared. We have to figure all of this out and we need to find that device. In the meantime, no one touches or disturbs this pattern, at least until we know what it is or what is says."

***

Aiko found herself sitting in a car. It was familiar as it belonged to her father in Japan. She did not know what kind of car it was and the details of it were blurred like a long off memory from a time she would not have noticed such details. She looked out, knowing that beyond the window was the lake, and the time that she remembered. Though the longing and the regret tugged at her, Aiko could feel herself relax. She did not even try to get out of the car, knowing full well that she could not. The lake was not actually there anymore.

She looked to her side to see her father at the driving seat. He was buckling up and whistling to himself. Before Aiko could say anything, a loud sound went off, waking her up instantly.

"Sam what's going on?" She said as she swung her legs over and got out of her bunk. "What's the alarm?"

"Fire?" Sam replied as Aiko took him off the cradle and put him on a movable module.

"Where?" Aiko replied, moving over to the wall and opening a panel to expose a fire extinguisher.

"Outside," Sam replied. "I am alerting the others now."

"Wait," Aiko said as she stopped, her brain still fuzzy from the dream. "That's impossible … there's next to no oxygen outside. A fire can't burn out there."

"That is not entirely true," Sam replied. "There is definitely a fire."

"Is it one of the modules?" Aiko asked as she ran toward one of the airlocks, meeting Mack and Havoc along the way.

"The modules are not touched," Sam replied. "It is a fire in the environment."

"Environment?" Aiko asked as she went into the bay, using one of the emergency suits, along with the two soldiers. "Wait … is it sector seventeen."

"Affirmative," Sam replied. "The strange marking is on fire."

"Coz, get your suit on and meet us in sector seventeen," Havoc ordered. "Bring your kit."

The trio made their way out of the airlock and into the Martian landscape. It was about an hour before sunrise and the temperatures were very low. There was no frost or moisture, but Aiko had learned what the terrain looked like in different temperatures. The sand was harder and more ridged.

Lights from the suits illuminated most of the path as there was little light coming over the horizon that teased the day to come. Aiko fought to control her breath, her heart still racing from the alarm wake up and her mind still struggling to sort out what was going on. As they came into sight of the module parked next to sector seventeen, they saw a bright light ahead of them. There was indeed a hot fire, casting bright glare onto the screens of the groups helmets.

"How is this possible?" Mack replied. "Doesn't fire need oxygen to burn?"

"There is a lot that can fuel a fire that is not oxygen," Sam said as he caught up with a large emergency module. "This appears to be a chemical fire. It can burn in zero oxygen until the materials have been exhausted."

"I can't believe it," Mack replied. "That's amazing."

"Not really," Havoc replied. "We've got a giant ball of fire floating in the center of our solar system that doesn't need oxygen to burn."

"I suppose you're right," Mack replied. "Are we going to put it out?"

"We are certainly going to try," Sam responded.

As the group got closer, Havoc stopped everyone about fifteen feet from the blaze. It appeared to cover the entire diameter of the design and was burning hot.

"My sensors show an incredible heat coming from the fire," Sam replied as he drove his module closer. "Please stand back."

"What is burning this?" Havoc asked. "I have never seen a fire like this in my life."

"It appears to have traces of fluorine, chlorine and various other chemical agents," Sam replied. "All things we have brought with us."

"Can you put it out?" Havoc asked.

"No," Sam replied. "It would take considerable amounts of fire suppression chemical and danger to this module. It makes more sense to let it burn out as it looks like it will only have another few moments of fuel left."

"It was one of us," Coz said as he approached in his suit. "All of these chemicals were mixed using ship stores."

"Who did this?" Havoc demanded. "Sam, pull the feed on the chemical stores, cameras, and door logs."

"Accessing," Sam replied. "That is odd. It seems that there has been a cascade failure in the logging computer."

"I'm on it," Aiko said as she took out her tablet and went to work. "You can destroy a log but there are backups for everything."

"There's only seven of us here," Havoc said, his tone frustrated. "It should not be very hard."

"The backups were switched off," Aiko admitted. "When the recording failure occurred, the backups were not recording."

"Who could have done that?" Mack asked. "That takes a lot of technical knowledge."

"I know," Aiko replied. "Sam and I are the only ones with the knowledge of the systems to pull something like that off."

"Well, that points the finger at you, doesn't it?" Coz replied.

"It isn't Aiko or Sam," Mack replied. "I have the room next to hers and her door was sealed all night."

"Are you sure?" Havoc replied.

"Yeah," Mack replied. "You know how light a sleeper I am."

"Sam would have access to other systems but nothing meticulous enough to make this while in remote," Havoc stated. "So that is myself, Aiko, Sam, and Mack who did not do this."

"Hey!" Coz replied. "How does Mack get an automatic out of suspicion? They are pretty tech savvy."

"So are you," Havoc replied. "Also, I trust Mack implicitly. If they told me you were an alien and I had to shoot you, I would believe them."

"Very funny," Coz replied. "You are joking, right?"

"Mack, is Coz an alien?" Havoc asked, his tone serious.

"He seems fine to me," Mack replied in a similarly serious tone. "No need to waste ammunition."

"Can we get back to the task at hand here?" Coz asked. "I was really looking forward to doing more experiments on that design and it looks like it is nothing but molten slag now."

"Right," Havoc nodded, getting back to task. "We cannot determine who had the technical expertise to cover their tracks. However, that leaves Prof, Ivy, and you. Who among who is left has the chemical expertise to pull this off?"

"We all do," Coz admitted. "This is like high school science level chemistry if you know how to do it. Prof, Ivy, and myself could easily have made this if we were so inclined."

"Do you have any way to vouch for not being part of this?" Havoc asked.

"Not that I can think of," Coz replied. "I was in my bunk all night and can't say I interacted with anyone after dinner last night."

"Any one of us see the others between then and now?" Havoc replied. "We need to get ahead of this."

The group looked at each other, no one offering anything.

"Ok, there has to be a way to see what happened that would not have been automatically recorded by the system," Havoc continued. "What about the suits? Can we figure out which ones had more oxygen depleted from them?"

"No," Aiko replied. "All of the suits were fixed into an automated system that refills them as needed."

"Does it keep a pressure log?" Havoc asked. "One that we can gauge."

"Yes," Aiko replied. "Though by using the emergency suits the oxygen system goes into emergency mode. Those logs immediately get overwritten."

"Footprints then?" Havoc replied, seeming to be grasping for straws.

"We all were out here yesterday at one point or another," Mack explained. "There would be no way to see which ones are freshest. Besides the suits all have the same size boot. They go over what we are wearing."

"Only Aiko wears smaller," Coz commented. "Though I am not sure that really matters."

"We need to think of motives then," Havoc replied. "Who would have the most reason to sabotage the pattern?"

"Well, we all would," Mack replied. "Ivy and Coz are being delayed in their experiments by moving to a new sector. Prof is seemingly unaffected by the delay, but could be acting to protect the crew."

Havoc sighed. "This is literally the worst place to have to be an arson detective. Mack, I want you to go back to HQ right now and round up Prof and Ivy. Search their quarters and see if there is any evidence you can find."

"On it captain," Mack said, heading back at once.

"What about me?" Coz replied. "You don't seriously think that I had any part of this?"

"What I think does not matter," Havoc replied. "I trust Mack and they exonerated Aiko and Sam. Beyond that is what I can see until I see otherwise. This is not a criminal investigation. There are no laws against burning alien symbols on Mars. We just need to know why, because this could lead to a bad situation if someone has to do this and cover their tracks."

"What about the aliens?" Aiko asked.

"What about them?" Havoc asked as he continued to watch the fire as it slowly burned out, having depleted all of the chemicals and oxidizing agents. "Is this what we should be thinking about now?"

"I think it very much should be," Aiko commented. "We have a very fragile relationship with these beings and they did something that could be called grandiose to interact with us."

"You think this pattern is … was a big deal to them?"

"As much as it was a big challenging idea to us to figure it out it must have also been to do it," Aiko commented. "This is the first direct interaction with the environment and before we even had a chance to decipher or respond to it, one of us destroyed it."

"Yeah that does sound bad," Havoc admitted.

"Imagine this was first contact with a race on Earth," Coz offered. "Like sailors to a new shore. The natives seem friendly and offer tributes in friendship since they do not know how to communicate. Imagine how it would look to them if the sailors then set fire to it?"

"Good point," Havoc replied. "Sam, I want you to use the module they communicate to us with and send a message. Tell them we meant no offense and not to take this as an insult."

"That will be difficult to translate to their understanding," Sam replied. "Wait … one moment."

"What is going on?" Havoc asked. "Sam?"

"I cannot communicate with the radio system of the module," Sam replied.

"Are they using it?" Aiko asked. "Is the computer system occupied?"

"No," Sam replied. "The systems are working through other communications. The radio system is offline. It appears that the radio system of the module has been tampered with."

"But that is our only direct line of communication with the aliens," Aiko replied.

"It appears that it has been sabotaged at the same time the fire was set," Sam replied. "I can of course replace this radio system but there is no guarantee that it will be recognizable to the aliens."

"They wanted to destroy the evidence of the aliens and cut us off from them," Havoc stated. "They seem to have done their job well."

"Well, we can only hope the aliens don't get too upset," Coz commented. "Because we are on their planet and we just slapped them in the face."

"Is there any other way to communicate with them?" Havoc asked. "Did we not get direct radio signals from the strange device?"

"Yeah, but we have no idea where on Mars that thing is," Coz replied.

"On Mars?" Aiko replied. "Didn't you say that thing resembled a strange Earth satellite? Sam, can you check space for it?"

"Checking," Sam replied. "There appears to be an unidentified object matching that description in an orbit near one of our assets. I cannot be sure, but it does seem like it is the device."

"We need to find a way to contact them," Havoc replied. "Because any species that can launch a satellite back to orbit without a rocket is not a one you really want to offend."

***

For the rest of the day, Havoc kept pretty much everything on lockdown as Mack and Sam did some investigations. Though the facility on Mars was an extremely high-tech installation, there were few redundancies that were not entirely necessary. This factor made it quite easy for someone to cover their tracks if they worked hard enough. On Earth, there was a lot of things that could leave traces behind, but in such a sterile environment like the facility and the near vacuum and barren wasteland beyond, it made for a perfect mix. Havoc gathered the entire crew to the meeting area. Everyone sat silent, all professing innocence.

"I want to go on record and say how disappointed I am," Havoc began. "One of us has proven untrustworthy and this throws our entire mission into jeopardy. This was a waste of vital supplies, a risk to our safety, and potentially a disaster we cannot even begin to understand the ramifications of. I am going to give the saboteur one chance and one chance only to come forward and tell me why they did it. This will be the only time I offer such with no ramifications. I only want a why and a promise to take no further rash action. You come forward right now and no official actions will be filed against you with NASA and mission control."

The room stayed silent, Aiko looked from Coz, to Prof, to Ivy, unwilling to believe any one of her colleagues could have done it. These people were her friends and she felt as though they had betrayed her. Though she was no more in charge of the alien situation as any, it had been her mission, her crusade, and now it was in jeopardy because of one person's rash actions.

"It seems that silence it is then," Havoc replied. "I am prepared for this eventuality. From now on every person, wears a tracker locator that will be real time linked with Sam. Someone here has proven untrustworthy, so we trust no one … that is how it has to be. Everyone will wear the locator and if you take it off or tamper with it, you answer to me. Is that understood?"

Everyone looked around, guilty and not guilty alike. No one liked the idea of the added measure, but it was what it has come to. Mack walked around and handed out a locator to each person, clipping it to their shirts.

"I never wanted this to be run like a military operation," Havoc said with a sigh. "I thought we were comrades, partners, and friends. However, now I must become the drill sergeant, the MP, the overseer. I now want everyone to run any major decisions past me before you do it or I will shut it down."

The group looked to Havoc all showing resentment and shame in the way events have turned out.

"Alright," Havoc nodded. "Now that we have that over, we need to focus. We will NOT be reclaiming sector seventeen for our use. We will continue to look for an alternative site for the work that was to be done there. Ivy and Coz will work on that while Prof takes restock of the supply of chemicals with Mack. We cannot be sure who took from our stores, but we do need to know precisely what we have left. As for Aiko, Sam, and myself, we are going to try our best to see if we can get into contact again with the aliens."

"We have had no response from the alien satellite, Captain," Sam replied. "It either cannot receive the messages or refuses to accept them."

"Where is it now Sam?" Aiko asked.

"It is nearing to being lined up with this site," Sam replied. "Should we try and contact it? Now would be the best time."

"Everyone, but those working with me, are dismissed," Havoc stated.

"But do we not have a right to witness anything to do with the aliens?" Prof asked.

"What if our expertise is needed?" Ivy chimed in.

"I said dismissed," Havoc said, turning his head and looking at Ivy and Prof with a frighteningly serious look on his face. "Do I need to repeat myself again?"

There were no more words said, the group, save for Sam and Aiko, leaving him behind in the meeting room.

"Ok," Havoc breathed out, his masculine tone of authority wavering. "That was fun."

"You don't like being the bad guy, do you?" Aiko asked.

"Good people never do," Havoc replied. "But some of them know that sometimes you have to be."

Aiko nodded. "I have been trying to contact the aliens. I have been broadcasting the same message on multiple frequencies."

"What is the message?" Havoc asked. "How did you sum up the situation?"

"Well, as you know, their understanding of our language might be good, but their understanding of our culture or morality is very primitive," Sam explained. "We needed to come up with the basest form of the idea so as to reach maximum understanding with as little room for misinterpretation possible."

"We went very simple," Aiko continued. "We made a mistake, please forgive us."

"Is that going to be enough?" Havoc asked. "Can we not tell them that one of us does not represent all of us?"

"That is much too complicated?" Sam replied. "We cannot even be sure they grasp the idea of a we as a plural. Humans are a very individualistic people. Each of us, though very technically similar, has a distinctive and unpredictable mind. For example, bees do as told and act very similarly to others. You would not expect one bee to spontaneously stop wanting to act like a bee for no reason. Humans however sometimes do the opposite of what is expected for seemingly random reasons."

"Also, telling them that one of us did something, but not all of us denotes an idea that we are inconstant." Aiko added. "It invites distrust as they cannot be sure who can be trusted and who cannot."

"What we sent to them is the simplest form of explanation," Sam continued. "It shows that we made a mistake and acknowledge that we did something wrong. Assuming they are rational in any semblance of their minds, they can understand that mistakes do get made and admitting to it is something that does not break trust."

"You are right," Havoc replied. "Though I wish it was a thing we could admit to ourselves more than to them."

"True," Aiko admitted. "It is hard to think that one of us would so something that might endanger us all."

"Well, they did it," Havoc replied. "We now need to focus on damage control."

"We are receiving a message!" Sam broke in. "Directly from the satellite."

"Relay it through your speech system," Aiko said, moving to the edge of her chair, her heart racing.

"You brought destruction," Sam replayed in a neutral tone. "Your mistake was great."

"We are sorry," Aiko relayed, looking to Havoc who seemed keen on letting Aiko do the talking. "Do you understand that we are confused as to how to communicate to you?"

"We thought you were like us," Sam replied. "We thought you came from the other twin."

"We come from that planet," Aiko replied. "But our peoples are very different. We are having issues understanding your people and part of us made a mistake as to your message."

"We understand your message," Sam replied. "We will respond similarly."

"We do not want our mistake to speak for us," Aiko pleaded. "We want another chance."

"They are no longer sending or receiving," Sam replied. "I think that statement was what they wanted us to know."

"What does that mean about our message?" Havoc asked. "How do they intend to respond to it?"

"Well, they called what we did as destruction," Aiko commented. "The message they got from us from it was that we liked to destroy things we did not understand. So, unfortunately, their response is that same message."

"That they will try and destroy what they don't understand?" Havoc asked.

"Precisely," Sam admitted. "I think we can expect some other form of action by them and this time it might prove a danger to the crew."

"This does provide an unfortunate dilemma," Havoc replied. "One that we are not exactly ready for,"

"Do you think we should contact mission control?" Aiko asked. "Get their recommendation?"

"What more would they be able to figure out from there that we can't here?" Havoc asked. "Mission control's only real recommendations would be to stay vigilant or abandon mission and head back to Earth."

"I would imagine that turning back to Earth, at this time, would be a foolish choice," Sam replied. "The ascension back to orbit takes considerable time and leaves us very venerable. The smallest tampering with the exit path can cause a catastrophic accident. On the surface, we can try and defend ourselves."

"You are talking about fighting them?" Aiko asked. "Like a war."

"I am a soldier, Aiko," Havoc replied. "Though I usually prefer more peaceful and reasonable solutions, I am trained and hard wired to meet force with force should it arise. If the aliens do indeed attack us, I will have to stop being your leader and become your protector."

"I hate that is seems to have come to this," Aiko commented. "First contact with life outside our home world and we are going to shoot space guns at it."

Havoc sighed. "I understand your concerns and no one wants this to be any different than me. I have only once had to turn to violence when diplomacy has failed and I know the price."

"What happened?" Aiko asked.

"There was an insurgency over an election in a country in Europe," Havoc replied. "The usual corrupt government, vote tampering and eventually it took a hacker to uncover the truth and set things right. However, a faction left over of those loyal to the previous government decided to stage a violent coup. They armed themselves as best they could and marched to a small town to hold it hostage. I was part of the peacekeeping force sent there to negotiate for their surrender and finally put an end to the hostilities."

"It went sideways on you?" Aiko asked.

"Very much so," Havoc replied. "We tried everything, negotiating, successions, compromise but it became very clear that these people did not want peace, they wanted control. They attacked us and surged forward to take our base of operations, a base filled with politicians, civilians, and non-combatants. My unit was forced to make a choice. The lives of the insurgents or the ones we protected. The fight only took twenty minutes, but when it was done, we took them out and saved not only the base but the village as well. However, though they called it a victory, my unit killed forty-seven people.

Though I never regretted my choice, I regret that it came to that in the first place. Should I have to show these aliens force, I will. I will protect every member of this crew with my life and, if it comes to it, I will stop at nothing to do it. I will regret meeting the first life off of Earth with violence but I will not regret the reason I will be forced to do it."

Aiko nodded. "I am sorry for questioning your reasoning. I regret it seems to have come to this."

"Force should always be questioned," Havoc agreed. "I will prepare for what I need to prepare for. You do whatever you can to prevent it. Should this go sideways on us, I don't want us to be able to say we did not try our best to prevent it."

***

Aiko again found herself in her father's car, it drove though the highway, surrounded by other cars as it went. She looked up at her father who looked bored, but concentrated on the mode.

"You know what is coming do you not?" Father asked. "It will not be very long now."

"The earthquake," Aiko commented, her adult mind peeking though. "We were on the highway when it happened. We were thrown around and we got into an accident. It was one of thousands of car accidents, but we were lucky. We got off the road with only minor damage to the car and without much injury."

"We were both relieved," Father replied, still driving as if he were on his way to a meeting with what was about to happen. "Though we had no idea how bad everything would go."

"Yes," Aiko commented. "It was not until we were safe on the side of the road and we thought of other places, like where we had come from. That is when we began to worry and things started to get so much worse."

"You wish you could change it all?" Father asked.

"Of course, I do!" Aiko replied. "This was the day that I lost everything!"

"What would you do?" Father asked. "How would you change it."

Aiko paused, all of the details and choices were in her head. She knew that even if she knew it was coming, there was not much she could do. No matter who she pleaded to or what she tried, she could not save her mother and her grandfather.

"I suppose there was nothing that I could do … I just wish that I would have tried."

"Tried to protect this moment?" Father asked.

"The moment, the people, the paradise," Aiko replied. "I miss it all and I would have protected it if I could have."

"You regret the destruction?" Father asked. "But you would do it again."

"Destruction?" Aiko asked. "What do you mean? That reminds me of …"

A buzzing sound awoke Aiko as she sat up and realized that she had slept at her desk. She had spent the night working on solutions, trying to find more ways to express their sentiments to the aliens, desperate to stop bad things from happening. The dream and what was said hung in her mind and proved to be elusive as many dreams. She looked down and saw that someone was trying to contact her.

Aiko reached down and hit the button on the com. "This is Aiko."

"This is Ivy," Ivy responded over the con. "The digging module I am using is having some issues. It seems to be stalling."

"Have you cycled the system?" Aiko asked, bringing up the modules data on her tablet.

"Did you just ask me if I turned it off and on?" Ivy asked.

"That is step number one in most technical support," Aiko replied. "It might fix it in this case."

"I have done it twice," Ivy replied. "It works for a few minutes, then starts to stall again."

"Alright," Aiko replied. "Nothing is showing up from this end, so I am going to come out and take a look at it in person. I will be there in fifteen."

"Confirmed," Ivy replied. "Thank you."

Aiko got her diagnostic gear together and went to the airlock to put on her spacesuit. She did not see Sam anywhere and assumed that he was hooked to one of his mobile modules. She hastily went through the checks and double checks of her suit before heading out. Aiko did not know when she got so used to wearing the spacesuit. She remembered when first she out one on during training and found it to be the most uncomfortable thing she had ever been in. The only doubts that she had about the mission were brought to the surface while in a spacesuit for the first time. However, lately she was fine with it, no more uncomfortable then being in a car. It was still a pain and time consuming, but it became routine like everything else. She walked through the dock and toward where Ivy was digging up a new spot.

As she came around one of the supply sheds she began to hear urgent static over the con.

"The modules going haywire!" Ivy shouted. "I can't control it."

Aiko began to run as fast as her spacesuit would allow, coming around the corner to see the massive cultivator module indeed acting erratically. It was spinning around on its massive tank tread core raising and lowering its digging arm that looked like an escalator with teeth. It collided with one of the light gantries, easily cutting through it and sending debris flying.

Ivy was on the other side of the area, taking cover by a group of crates and supplies.

"Havoc, we have an issue in sector eight," Aiko said over the comm but received back nothing but static. "Havoc? Mack? Sam? Anyone come in?"

"Some sort of interference!" Ivy shouted back. "Only local comm seems to be working."

"Ok, stay where you are," Aiko said as she ducked next to the shed. The module seemed to be moving on its treads but not directly toward herself or to ivy.

"We need to stop the module!" Ivy shouted. "It's the only one we have."

"It's too dangerous," Aiko commented. "Even a glancing blow will rip open our suits. As long as it stays away from anything vital, we should be fine. It only has so much power before it needs to re-charge."

"It's coming this way!" Ivy shouted.

Aiko looked out and indeed saw the module make a turn toward Ivy, the digging arm swung, narrowly missing Ivy and taking the top right off of the large crate she was hiding behind.

Aiko did not think. She did not plan. She simply ran toward the module as fast as she could. She knew that there was a human height control panel off to the side and, if she could access it, she could manually power off the system. The cultivator arm swung out again, moving in the direction Aiko was running. She dove to the ground and could feel the vibrations from it in her suit as it passed just inches above her. Once it was clear she got up, struggling to run again and close more distance toward the module. She felt fear. She could feel every detail of what would happen should the module touch her with the razor-sharp digging prongs. Aiko's heart raced, the adrenaline took over and gave her ultra-keen focus on what she had to do and think of nothing else.

She reached the control panel and smacked her spacesuit off of it so hard it left a small spider web crack on the front of her helmet. She shrugged it off. She had work to do. She hastily removed the control panel, exposing the manual controls. The digital readout seemed to be glitching, waves of interference going over it and making any usage of the system impossible. Aiko gave up on control and instead yanked the whole screen out. She knew there was a manual override panel beyond and she could plug her wrist mounted device into it. She hastily pulled a wire, connecting it to her wrist and going in for manual analog access.

"Aiko, hurry," Ivy shouted. "I'm out in the open. I have nowhere to go for cover."

"I'm almost there," Aiko replied. "Just giving the shutdown code."

"Module manual shutdown procedure engaged," the system said over the local con. "Full shut down in sixty seconds."

"Sixty seconds?" Aiko asked. "Damn BriarTech OS bullshit."

Aiko was startled from her condemnation of the system as the massive tank treads of the module began to move. She was forced to scramble back, lest she got caught up and crushed. As she got some distance, she realized she was now within the gantry swing of the cultivator arm and very exposed. The module, as if noticing somehow she was venerable, stopped its swing and turned around. The arm began to lower as it swung, coming right for Aiko in a trajectory she could not hope to dodge.

Aiko knew what was coming and could only hope it would be over quickly. She knelt down and braced herself, closing her eyes so she did not see it coming. However, mere seconds before impact she felt a rumbling behind her and the crashing of metal on metal. She opened her eyes to see the gantry arm mere feet from her position, the razor-sharp cultivator prongs seeming hung up on something. She turned her body to look what had stopped it and saw that another module, a drilling rig, had rolled over and stopped the arm with one of its drill arms.

"Please forgive my lateness," Sam said over the local comm. "Interfacing with one of these directly is not as easy as you would think."

"Sam!" Aiko shouted. "You saved me."

"Not yet I haven't," Sam replied. "Please get clear."

Aiko scrambled away, out of the reach of the gantry arm as the drill module released it. The cultivator arm moved as if to swing again but it began to jerk and slow down. Within seconds the power began to go out, soon leaving the module dead in the water.

Ivy ran over to Sam and Aiko. "What was that? What happened to the cultivator?"

"It would appear as some sort of errant and malignant code got into its automated systems. It took over its orders and drove it to a frenzy."

"Are you in danger?" Aiko asked. "Can the code hurt you?"

"Not a chance," Sam replied. "I am more like a human than I am a computer. I have the ability to reject code and commands."

"Was this the aliens?" Ivy asked, ear clear on her voice. "Are they trying to kill us over what we did to the pattern?"

"Undetermined," Sam replied. "I cannot yet figure out where this errant code has come from. We cannot rule out that it is not from the aliens."

"It was going right for us," Ivy commented. "It was trying to kill Aiko and I."

"This is Havoc," Havoc said over general comm. "What is going on over there?"

"It would appear that full comm is back online," Sam replied.

"One of the modules went haywire," Aiko commented. "It would appear as though it was trying to attack Ivy and myself."

"I am on my way," Havoc asked. "Is anyone hurt?"

"We are fine," Aiko commented. "I have minor damage to my helmet and will require a patch kit for the return to the airlock. Ivy is uninjured and her suit is not compromised. The cultivator module took damage and will need a full system diagnostic before we even consider turning it back on again. The cultivator damaged gantry structures and supply crates, we will have to assess it all later."

"Drilling module took minor damage," Sam added. "The composite alloy drill bit took most of the stress and is undamaged."

"We will worry about Aiko's suit first," Havoc replied. "Do not move until I get there with the patch kit. Stay alert and keep an eye on everyone's backs. This might just be them carrying through on their threat."

"They threatened us?" Ivy asked.

"They said they would answer destruction with destruction," Aiko commented.

"Well, they were not kidding," Ivy replied as she looked at the module and all that it had destroyed. "This surely is destruction."

"We were lucky," Sam replied. "No loss of life and no critical systems damaged. We can only hope that this makes us even."

Chapter Five: Surrounded Yet Alone

There have been many accidents in space, times where a very simple failure or miscalculation caused an issue that proved disastrous for all involved. It was very easy that a faulty part or an honest mistake took the lives of many in but an instant. The team on Mars had their first accident and luckily no one had been killed. Sam and Havoc secured the zone as Aiko made sure the module was off and rigged unusable until an examination could be done. After the dust had settled and everything seemed to be safe for the time being, the group met up to discuss with mission control what was going on.

"So, let me get this straight," Joy began her summary. Unlike her name her tone was completely devoid of Joy. "There was some manner of message burnt into the sand, made of glass. Before you could even begin to decider it, someone who you cannot determine burnt it to nothing."

"Affirmative," Havoc confirmed, looking to the group with frustrated eyes reminding them of his frustration and disappointment.

"The … other factor showed dismay over this act," Joy continued. "Then without warning the cultivator module went haywire and seemed to be trying to kill members of the crew?"

"Yes," Havoc replied.

There was a long pause before Joy continued, "And you believe that it was the others that did this?"

"Sam and Aiko did a thorough investigation," Havoc replied. "We are still searching for all of the answers."

"What did you uncover?" Joy asked. "Of the attack with the module?"

"Well we determined that someone had patched into it and taken it from automatic control to manual," Aiko replied. "Sam and I do not know how they did it but they seemed to be controlling it in real time."

"The thing was gunning for us!" Ivy added. "It was both deliberate and terrifying."

"You believe that this was the … aliens trying to prove a point?" Joy asked.

"The aliens did refer to what we did as destruction," Havoc replied. "And they would do as we did."

"I am not convinced that this was intentional on their part," Aiko commented.

"You were there!" Ivy snapped. "The thing nearly killed you!"

"It just doesn't add up for me," Aiko commented. "We did not kill any of them as far as they have said or we can determine. Death is a step up from destruction and an escalation contrary to their threat."

"Contrary to their threat?" Ivy commented, her tone one of disbelief. "A threat of violence is a threat of violence. Just because one is more severe than the other it doesn't make it less a damn threat of violence!"

"Ivy is right," Joy replied. "Severity does not make it not an act of violence against us."

"Yes, but you need to understand how detailed this attack would be for them," Aiko continued. "We have proven that they have issues perceiving us as what we are. Do you seriously think they can figure out how best to hurt us? I think their threat meant that they were going to destroy something, not us."

"How could they not know how to hurt us?" Ivy asked. "We are the squishy ones that need suits to live."

"They might not even know we aren't the modules," Aiko replied. "There are literally dozens of machines roaming around they can communicate with. They might not know that we are even carbon based biological beings."

"Could the act have been meant to damage the module and not us?" Prof weighed in. "Perhaps that was the real target."

"No! Not possible," Ivy shouted. "The thing went for Aiko and she ducked an attack. The next time it got a chance it came at an angle she could not duck. It was going for us and getting increasingly better at it."

"I would be inclined to agree with Ivy on this one," Joy replied. "Despite what was intended they reacted with what was from us only an act of vandalism with a show of force with the intent to kill. I speak for mission control on the idea that if it comes down to an 'Us versus them' scenario we are to proceed with the full force to defend our assets."

"What are your orders?" Havoc asked, his tone official and serious.

"Frist of all secure all mechanical assets they might also use to attack," Joy began. "Then set up a defensive perimeter and prepare to meet any show of the aliens as a potential threat."

"So, wipe them out if they show themselves?" Aiko asked. "Is that what this has come down to?"

"Aiko, I find it rather curious that you are not taking the situation as seriously as it deserves," Joy replied. "Your life was at risk as much as Ivy's and you are championing the cause of not defending ourselves."

"I never said I do not want us to defend ourselves," Aiko clarified. "I just mean that you guys are acting like this is a war we have up here."

"Isn't it?" Joy asked. "We are on their planet and they tried to kill members of our people. That sounds like war to me."

"But we are on their planet," Aiko replied. "Does this not mean that we cannot be the aggressors here?"

"That would be the ideal situation," Joy confirmed. "But this situation has proven far short of ideal. They have proven their desire for aggression and we are reacting to meet it."

"Well we started it," Aiko commented. "Someone up here seems to want to fight with them."

"We have no way of knowing who it was according to the captain," Joy replied. "That being so, we have to focus on what we do know and that is that they hold the potential of violence. Our orders stand. We focus on the safety and continuation of the mission."

Joy and mission control signed off, leaving the group in silence wondering what would come next. Over the next few days there were no signs of the aliens nor were there any further incidents. As Sam used a repair module to repair the damaged equipment, Aiko worked to put added safeguards in place to prevent it from happening again. She put in a failsafe inside the computers that logged in the control code of whoever used it. She set it so if it were not her or Sam who was outing in a command it would alert her in her tablet. That way she could kill power to any module should she discover it was not something one of the others meant for it to do that was part of the mission. She decided not to tell anyone about that just yet even though there were people she trusted she did not trust them not to be sloppy with the information. Whoever was tampering with logs and performing espionage knew how to cover their tracks and the less they knew of her new security measures the better.

The cultivation module was the harder of the two damaged modules to fix but soon was back online with the driller. Things began to get back to normal, everyone continuing the work to try to get some headway to the already messed up schedule.

Aiko liked being busy. It seemed to make the time fly by and time that flew kept her mind off other things. She knew all the evidence was that the aliens were responding to what was going on with violence but it didn't feel right to her. Though it was just a hunch she did not want to let it go. She did not ever feel like the aliens wanted war or wanted to fight but she had no way to prove it.

Aiko pulled up the aerial photograph of the now destroyed glass markings. No one on the crew had any idea how to decipher it and it frustrated her. This message was a lost piece of a puzzle and Aiko knew that if she could figure it out it might lead to answers.

Prof entered the lab, stopping to look up at the symbol portrayed on the screen.

"I don't believe they want to hurt us either," he said.

Aiko looked back and smiled.

"They are certainly upset with us but I think there is more to it," Aiko responded.

"Is that why you are staring at this thing?" Prof asked as he sat down. "You think that if we could respond to this they might be … less upset."

Aiko nodded, "This could very much be a question … a serious one. What if it meant something like *Welcome to Mars?* Imagine the insult by our destroying it. They don't now we can't figure this out. All they know is we destroyed it."

"And they have been ignoring us as a result?" Prof asked. "Well at the very least."

"Wait!" Aiko said, ideas formulating in her mind. "They have never outright refused to talk to us before."

"Yeah," Prof agreed. "I have gone on all of the recorded correspondence and they have seemed rather eager with our responses, even ones they didn't like or understand."

Aiko nodded as she pulled out the last text they had gotten from the aliens.

"Ok I have an idea here and I want your opinion," Aiko put forth.

"You got it," Prof replied. "I am fascinated by these aliens and I very much want to give them the benefit of the doubt. What do you have?"

"Ok these aliens do not have the same perception of life as we do," Aiko commented. "At the very least they cannot express it quite like we do."

"Agreed," Prof replied.

"Well what if by destruction they don't mean of us or anything of ours?" Aiko asked.

"Then how did they mean it?" Prof replied. He was not quite sure what Aiko was suggesting.

"Well when they communicate with us they use a lot of ideas that are not very definite," Aiko continued. "They are interpreting our ideas as they see them and formatting their responses to something they think we can understand."

"A lost in translation kind of thing?" Prof agreed. "But what was it they were truly trying to say."

"Well the symbol wasn't really anything to them that they valued," Aiko replied "It was a message, a more direct line of thought. They said something to us and we destroyed the message."

"We destroyed the communication," Prof suggested. "So, they will destroy communication too."

"They didn't mean they would destroy us," Aiko agreed. "They will stop communicating with us as we think we don't want to communicate with them."

"So, when they debated about the … fire … they thought we were debating whether we wanted to keep talking to them or not?" Prof asked.

"Yes," Aiko nodded. "And they decided to make our decision for us and just cut off communication."

Prof nodded, "Can we go to the others? Perhaps this will ease things?"

"I doubt it," Aiko admitted. "They are pretty rattled, pretty much the whole crew. We will need something better than how we interpret things."

"Then what can we do?" Prof asked. "How can we get them to realize that we indeed want to talk to them again?"

"We need to respond to the message," Aiko said as she looked back to the pattern. "We need to answer this question we can't understand."

"Then let's figure it out," Prof responded. "We figure out what this message was supposed to be and we can fix this whole situation."

"Sam spent hours going over this," Aiko replied as she scrolled though the log of all his tests. "It's not language, math, constellations, its practically gibberish."

"What if it isn't really a message or question in the strictest sense," Prof asked as he walked up to the screen. What if it is an interpretation of an idea or an expression of art?"

"Art?" Aiko asked in a skeptical tone. "Like they want to show us their creativity."

"Well they seem to be figuring out we interpret things visually," Prof replied. "So, they made a great visual idea to show us."

"Yes, but how do we decipher it," Aiko said. "It doesn't look like anything to me."

"Ok Aiko I want us both to close our eyes," Prof suggested as he closed his.

"What is the point?" Aiko asked. "Sam's are infinitely better than ours and he saw nothing."

"Trust me," Prof asked again, his eyes still closed. "Sam is a genius of engineering but he doesn't have a human's ability to interpret things on instinct."

"Alright," Aiko said as she closed her eyes. "What now?"

"We count to three," Prof instructed. "And when we do so we both open our yes and say the first thing that pops into our head that it looks like. Treat it like a Rorschach and let our instincts guide us."

"Ok," Aiko replied. "Let's give it a shot."

"Good," Prof said as he took a breath. "One…two…three."

Both Aiko and Prof opened their eyes and for a split-second Aiko saw something, an idea, something the gibberish image reminded her of. Both Prof and Aiko shouted out what they saw and it just happened to be the same word. They both looked to each other in disbelief, not just that they had said the same word but the word made sense. It was what the image was trying to portray and now that they saw it they could not un see it.

"What do we do now?" Prof asked.

"Sam come in," Aiko said in response. "We know what the pattern in the sand was … it's a cell!"

***

Sam came with his module and analyzed both the information from Prof and Aiko as well as all the archived knowledge on cells in his databanks. He worked slowly and Aiko could hear the processing power of his spherical head go over terabytes of information each second. When it stopped, she knew that he was formulating his findings and was about to offer a hypothesis.

"I cannot be sure," Sam responded. "But I think you have indeed cracked it."

"So, it is a cell?" Prof asked with a smile.

"It appears to be one," Sam replied. "Though keep in mind that it is not exactly one that we have on record. This is a cell by the loosest definition of cells that we can determine."

"What is so different about it?" Aiko asked.

"Well the cells of all life on earth is of a similar design," Sam began. "Even creatures and life forms so divergently different all share similar cells in how they were made. All cells on Earth are based upon carbon binding to other elements and creating connections that bonded to oxygen to create life. If this is to be understood it seems that they are from silicon similarly binding to other atoms and attracting carbon dioxide to create life."

"So, this cell is the simplest building block of all life here?" Prof asked.

"Precisely," Sam replied. "They realize that our two life forms are very different from each other and to try to bridge our understanding they are … or were, showing us the most basic part of what they are."

"Then the right way to respond would be with something similar," Aiko responded. "Can we make an image like theirs but show them our carbon-based cell?"

"One moment," Sam replied, the image of the alien pattern on the screen was then replaced with a similar looking pattern. "Using the picture of the illustration they presented to us I kept all the structure the same and changed the parts. It was relatively easy once we knew how to do it."

"So, if they looked at this they would understand what manner of life forms we are?" Prof asked.

"Presumably yes," Sam replied. "That seemed to be the question and this seems to be the answer."

"Do you think they will be happy with this?" Prof asked. "Do you think it would fix things?"

"That I have no idea," Sam replied. "Though the aliens have a workable understanding of our technology and language there is no way to gauge their mindset."

"Agreed," Aiko replied with a sigh. "They can mimic and reconcile our words but their emotions are … pardon the term … alien to us. We have no way of knowing how long or even if they could hold a grudge."

"Well I say we give it a shot," Prof asked. "Best case we open the line of communication again. Worst case we are where we are right now."

"I do not know if anyone else will go for it," Sam admitted. "Even Havoc who was pretty on board with alien contact seems to be in war mode because of the accidents."

"I still do not think the aliens did it," Aiko replied.

"Well if they didn't that means that one of us did it," Prof replied. "And I find that very hard to deal with even if I believe it."

"Well there is a lot of secrets and lies going on," Aiko admitted. "This situation has snowballed and I will not let it continue to do so when the answer might present itself. Sam, if I asked you to help me would you do it or would you be obligated to tell Havoc and mission control?"

"I am permitted to make a judgement call based on the safety of the mission," Sam replied. "Prof does make a fair point in that showing them our cell symbol would not make things worse and could potentially make it better. Though I would be obligated to tell Havoc my direct involvement I am not in control of what would happen to the symbol that is left in the drive of the projector. I have no control if someone uploads it to a portable laser cutter. I also have no control over someone taking it and using it to carve into a rock or otherwise hardened surface."

"Thank you, Sam," Aiko said with a smile.

"Thank you for what?" Sam said as he powered up his mobile module and started to roll away. "All I did was state where things were and how they might work."

Prof watched Sam leave then walked back over to Aiko, "Will it work?"

"The auto laser cutter?" Aiko asked as she began to upload it to the device. "It is certainly well within the specs for the device. It is meant to do custom cutting or scoring as well as excavate samples from the rock. All we would have to do is bring a tripod and set it up and it will score the symbol."

Prof nodded, "The big problem is where we would put it. As mentioned we have no idea how these aliens see or perceive information. We could put it on the ground right now and have no way to even know if they could see it until they spoke to us."

"We could put it on or near the site where they put ours," Aiko suggested. "They must be at least aware of things on that spot."

"It could be an insult," Prog suggested. "We destroyed theirs and put ours overtop. Also, mission control and Havoc have that area under tight surveillance."

"Yeah that leads us to another problem," Aiko commented. "We had someone sabotage the last message and there's no telling if they would sabotage this one. We would have to go out, place it somewhere where they will see it and without our own crew seeing it."

Prof sighed, "Yeah and Havoc has us on a short leash at the moment. To take the laser and a tripod out we will need to tell him why and them BAM, everyone knows."

"It is not exactly ideal," Aiko admitted. "I have no idea what to do."

"Well I have volunteered as a doctor is some really dangerous places," Prof replied. "We heard once of an outbreak of a sickness in a nearby village, something we had the antibiotics and resources to fix easily. The issue was that it was deep in a restricted zone and we were told that such a mission was impossible. However, the next day it turned out some troops were being sent out to survey a place within a mile of the village. We volunteered to accompany them in case of injury or attack and easily snuck off, dropped off the medical supplies and instructed the villages how to use it all. The outbreak was halted and we did so without arousing suspicion or breaking orders. We just have to wait until a mission or operation takes us somewhere where we could deploy the symbol and do it."

"Who knows how long that could take?" Aiko asked. "We need to …"

"Aiko to the seismic control bay," Havoc said over the con. "We need you to take a look at something."

"On my way," Aiko replied.

"This could lead to something," Prof replied. "Are we that lucky?"

"I guess we are going to find out," Aiko smiled as she grabbed her tablet and headed out to meet with Havoc in the seismic control bay.

As she entered she saw Coz, Ivy, and Havoc standing around the controls. The room was a large control station that coordinated various information from seismic probes and cultivation modules.

"What's going on?" Aiko asked as she joined the group.

"Before we say anything can you do a diagnostic and confirm the seismic controls are functioning perfectly?"

"Absolutely," Aiko said, taking out some tools from her belt and connecting her tablet. It took several moments but soon she got green lights all around. "The seismic controls are working well within optimal specifications. So, what is this about?"

"Ok we had to check," Havoc replied. "Because we think we found something."

"An alien something?" Aiko guessed, knowing that only topics to do with the aliens were described so vaguely.

"We were doing seismic scans to an area nearby," Coz replied. "Though there are many caverns and holes in the crust in this region this one appears deliberate."

"Define deliberate?" Aiko asked.

Coz hit some keys and brought up a three-dimensional seismic scan. It seemed to portray a series of circular tunnels.

"This is it."

"I still think it could be naturally occurring," Ivy said as she crossed her arms.

"Have you ever heard of Giotto di Bondone?" Coz asked.

"I fail to see how this relates," Ivy replied with a skeptical look.

"Giotto di Bondone was a famous artist and painter in the late middle ages," Coz began. "He was once asked to prove his artistic talent to the pope. He simply drew a freehand circle on a piece of paper and sent it. All who looked at it were shocked by how he had drawn what looked to all as a perfect freehand circle. Such perfection is rare in naturally occurring phenomena and I have analyzed this circle and it is indeed perfect. Only we with our tools and science can recreate such a thing."

"Yes, but that is just an anecdote," Ivy added. "It proves nothing."

"It proves enough to make it worth a look," Havoc replied. "Aiko what do you think."

"I'd like to take a look," Aiko replied. "I can use the portable laser cutter to get some samples."

"Sounds good," Havoc agreed. "I will run it past mission control and put a team together."

Ivy slowly nodded, "I will go as well, you will need me on this. Best case this is nothing and we have an interesting hole to take samples from, worst case … well at least we will finally know where they are."

***

The trip to the source of the strange circular cave did not take as long as the one to the original resting place of the strange black satellite. It was only a couple of hours by rover until Mack, Coz, Ivy, Sam and Aiko were at the coordinates indicated by the seismic computer. The area looked like any other with flat red hardened sand and looked featureless compared to anything in the near vicinity.

The group got out of the rover, collected their equipment and walked out onto the sandy pitch.

"Are we sure we got the right place?" Coz asked. "This looks like nothing really."

"Coz you really do like to focus on what is in front of you," Ivy scolded. "It's below silly."

"I was just being clever in the face of what could be a full alien civilization," Coz commented. "How do we get in?"

"We need to find an easy way in that doesn't disturb too much," Aiko added. "We want to knock, not kick in the front door."

"There appears to be a thin area of upper silicon over here," Sam said as he rolled a rather large module over to the side. "I can easily cut through and there is a gradual incline below."

"A slope," Ivy commented. "That should work."

Sam went to work, using a cutting arm to open a hole big enough for the others to walk through wearing their bulky space suits. Within moments the group began down the slope to the cavern below. Each astronaut and Sam turned on their lights, revealing a smooth tunnel that looked like it was part of the terrain.

"This was not cut," Ivy commented. "It looks like it was grown."

"Just like the glass pattern it looks like it took some level of sophisticated control beyond our current level of scientific complexity."

"In other words, you have no clue how they did it?" Ivy replied with a smirk.

"As much as I hate to admit it," Coz replied. "That is pretty accurate."

"It doesn't look like anyone is home?" Ivy commented. "Someone built this but where are they?"

"It looks as though the area is circular. It has many offshoots and divergent paths," Aiko said as she looked at the seismic scan. "Maybe we should all look around."

"Do you think that is wise?" Mack replied. "Splitting up?"

"Well we all have maps that can lead us back to this position in real time," Aiko replied. "Sam can co-ordinate if anyone gets lost."

Mack sighed, "Ok, everyone go a different path but we meet up back here in ten whether we find anything or not."

Everyone agreed and went off in search of anything they could find. Aiko picked a path and begun walking.

"Sam what do you make of this place?" Aiko asked.

"It is hard to say really," Sam replied over the con. "It is difficult to date things here, especially with us not knowing how they make places like this. It could be ancient or it could be brand new. We do not yet have a metric to gauge such things."

"It seems the more we discover about this life form the less we figure out," Aiko replied, walking through the tunnels, trying to place anything out of the ordinary … or at least more out of the ordinary than everything else. "They built this place with what looks like a lot of effort and care, but it seems abandoned. Are you picking up anything here at all?"

"The scans are inconclusive," Sam replied. "Since everything here seems based on a level of silicon on silicon it is like finding a needle in a haystack but the needle is made of hay."

"That is a really good analogy," Aiko commented.

"Thank you," Sam replied. "It is based on a small amount of irony to illicit the idea of a nearly impossible goal."

"Not so impossible," Aiko replied. "I am a detail oriented person with near infinite patience. I am the kind of person that could catalogue every part of that haystack till that needle is found."

"Of that I have no doubt," Sam replied. "I must see to another crewmember I will be back."

Sam went silent on the comm as Aiko came to a nexus of several paths. She had seen no sign of life, no indicator of life that still dwelled here.

"Ok, I am hoping that you guys just moved but at least know this is still here," Aiko said.

Aiko took out the tripod to the laser cutter and set it up near the center of the large nexus. She attached the laser cutter and powered it up. She set it to go and stepped back to give it the space to work. It warmed up and shot a series of beams from its lenses and began to laser cut the large detailed cell symbol into the ground. She had no way of knowing if it would be effective, or even if it would be seen but this was her best option.

Aiko checked her time, realizing that she was cutting it close as the device did its work. The last thing she needed was Ivy or Coz to come and see what she had done. The machine was nearly finished and she calculated the time it would take to break down the device and head back … it would be close. But before she could even start work the ground shook and the force knocked her to the ground, toppling over the tripod and shutting down the laser.

"Sam, what was that?" Aiko asked over the comm.

"There appears to have been some manner of explosion," Sam replied. "Come to the extraction point at once."

"I need to collect the laser," Aiko replied as she got up and walked over to it.

"The tunnel is becoming unstable," Sam replied. "Many paths are collapsing … leave it!"

Aiko got up and turned from the laser. She moved as fast as she could in her suit, keeping careful watch on her wrist mounted screen so she would not get lost. She soon rounded the corner to encounter a thick layer of debris and dust. She could see lights dancing around in the semi-darkness but could not figure out which direction was correct. She looked at her wrist display but could barely see it in the dust.

A hand grabbed her, it was Mack, "This way."

They dragged Aiko and soon the light from the surface could be seen permeating through.

Aiko climbed up and collapsed onto the ground above. She fought to catch her breath from both the exertion and the fear. She looked around, seeing Sam's module helping Ivy patch up part of her suit and Mack standing next to her, examining their and Aiko's suit for damage.

"Where is Coz?" Aiko said, looking around.

"A cave in got him," Mack replied, their tone official and devoid of emotion. "I could not get to him."

"Sam!" Aiko shouted. "Can you link to his suit, his comm and life signs, link them to my display."

"I really would prefer not," Sam replied. "You will not like the information that I am receiving."

"Is his suit breached?" Aiko replied. "Is there damage?"

"His suit is destroyed," Sam admitted. "Though I am getting signals from Coz's suit it has become decompressed and all life signs have ceased."

"We got to get to him," Aiko replied as she slowly stood. "We got to dig him out … he could still be …"

"He's gone," Mack said as they put a hand on Aiko's shoulder. "You know as well as I how long you survive here without a suit. Even if he were somehow alive we would never get to him in time and even if we did we don't have the facilities here to even ty to revive him."

"How can you be so heartless?" Ivy demanded. "He was a friend."

"Because I have to be!" Mack snapped. "You are my friends too and if I allowed you to try and go back down there I would lose you too. You think this is easy for me?"

Aiko took a deep breath, it was not easy for her any more than Ivy but she allowed her logical mind to start updating with the facts. "We cannot do any more for him here. Sam what is the seismic stability here? Are we safe?"

"Hard to tell," Sam replied. "There have been many collapses underground and this area could become unstable at any time."

"Alright we are getting out of here," Mack ordered. "Back to the rover and we head back to base. We can figure everything out when we get there."

In a few hours, the group was back at base camp. Ivy, Mack, and Aiko sat down in the meeting area and Prof brought them hot drinks. Coffee was a luxury and something they did not expect to find on Mars but it appeared Prof had smuggled some on board and now seemed a good a time as any to share.

Aiko looked around as everyone gathered, her mind half expecting Coz to just march in and make some kind of sarcastic remark. She had to remind her brain that it would be something that would never happen again and this drove the point home and made it hurt all the more.

Havoc walked in, taking a cup of coffee from Prof and taking a drink. He sighed slightly, both from seeming to try to enjoy the coffee and the realization to what he had to do next.

"I don't think I need to tell you this is literally the hardest part of command. No matter the challenges or setbacks there is nothing harder than having to discuss the loss of someone who served with you to others that care about them. I will not beat around the bush, we are a small group and there is no way for any of us not to know what happened. We all need to grieve and we all need to come to terms with it but first and foremost we need answers. We need to know what happened," Havoc said to the group.

"They hit us," Ivy replied. "We went to their home and they kicked us out with force."

"Do we have any evidence what caused this?" Havoc asked. "Was it them?"

"Who else could it have been?" Mack asked.

"Well I realize that with all of this it is easy to forget that we might have a saboteur," Havoc replied.

"You honestly think one of us would have done this?" Ivy replied. "One of us might have killed Coz?"

Havoc sighed, "No … that is the least likely scenario. Sam, could you please determine what caused the explosion."

"Inconclusive," Sam replied. "The explosion happened inside the cavern and collapsed it as it went. Most of the cave-ins were caused by a chain reaction and we have no sensors that can determine what it is. The evidence to what caused the explosion is unfortunately buried now."

"I am not sending any more assets … friends out there," Havoc stated. "We need to focus on a more realistic scenario."

"And what is that?" Ivy asked.

"Well as with the other issue there are two causes for this," Havoc began. "Either one of us caused the explosion as sabotage and it went wrong or the aliens stuck at us with intent to kill. Either way the outcome is the same."

"How so?" Aiko asked. "There are always a lot of options."

"It is about outcome," Havoc explained. "That the alien attacks will continue."

"How could you possibly know that?" Aiko asked. "Perhaps by doing nothing we can protect ourselves?"

"Well let's look at it like this …" Havoc continued. "If say one of us blew it up … that's another mark against us for them to respond to … leads to escalations we need to defend against. If they blew it up it shows that they are at least capable of killing one of us and that can lead to escalation we need to defend against. Either way you look at it we must hunker down, fortify the base and prepare for the worst."

Aiko sighed, she wanted to debate but even she found herself doubting the aliens and putting intent upon them.

"You can count on me," Aiko responded.

"Good," Havoc replied with a nod. "We do what we can to defend the base and once we get a bead on it we will get together and say a few words for Coz. Dismissed."

The group all left as if they were on autopilot. They were on an alien world and though there will still people left, all seemed to feel so desperately alone.

**

Aiko worked as hard as she had become accustomed to since arriving on Mars but something now felt different. All of her convictions, all of her ideas of the infinite possibility of what they could do were drastically diminished. When she had arrived, she thought she had found discovery and wonder but instead only found secrets and death. She helped set up a perimeter around the base that sent a weak electric current through the sand and rock. It would alert them in real time against anything from below or the sand itself that might hurt them. She still did not believe that the aliens were the ones that killed Coz but she had neither the evidence to prove it nor the true desire to look at the alternative.

The others had done what they could to fortify the camp, all semblance of the work and the mission seemed to be on hold. Aiko overheard discussion with Mack and Havoc about weapons and potential ways to fight. Aiko was glad they had not asked her to be involved, admitting she would not know how to hurt them even if she wanted to.

She stared at her screen at her workstation, her eyes blurring and her head fuzzy. She realized that she should probably get some sleep. Normally she fought an internal battle with her mind about sleep, being a workaholic and pushing her body and fatigue as far as it would usually go. However, now she knew that her brain was too diluted with other things and rest was really her only option to have any hope of clearing it. She went to her small quarters and looked to the portable cradle Sam usually recharged in. He was not there, busy with one module or another. Aiko could not help but lament to the time on the voyage here where Sam was like her constant companion and where she went he usually went as well. She also lamented this as the trip here seemed to be filled with wonder and opportunity. She longed to feel that good about things again but knew there was no way to return to it.

She climbed into her bunk and settled in. She thought it would take her time to fall asleep, time to reconcile things enough to relax but instead found her eyes leaden and her body ready to have fallen asleep hours ago.

She looked at the mountains. Her father once told her the names of them all but she had forgotten. She could feel shaking and vibrations at her feet, aftershocks not as bad as the first big shakes but still concerning. She stared at the mountains because she was told to.

"Just keep looking at the mountains Aiko," Father said, his voice troubled and obviously hiding concern. "You just keep looking at those mountains, they are huge and unmoving. They won't go anywhere."

Aiko stared at the mountains, following her father's words and finding some solace. Her adult mind flowed forward as she realized that she was reliving a memory.

"I remember this. The ground shook and we crashed and got off the road. I was so scared but you had things to do."

Aiko could feel her childlike terror as to what was going on behind her but decided to ignore it and turn around. She saw a calamity of horror and chaos behind her. Hundreds of cars, many crashed and a few on fire. She and her father had been on the highway when the big quake hit and the result was pandemonium. She saw her father, only a few feet away, performing first aid on a crash victim that had been thrown from a car. Behind them was the family of the fallen woman, all battered but standing and watching Aiko's father fight to save one of their own. The woman on the ground was bloody and injured very badly, looking to have been thrown several feet from the car on impact. Father had not wanted Aiko to see what he was doing, trying to spare her from the blood and violence. However, he could not allow her to wander farther so he had invented the idea of staring at the mountains.

"I suppose that is where I got it," Aiko said with a laugh, the horror around her coming into perspective of being a memory and not real. "The idea of focusing on something that cannot change to ignore the idea of what change is forced upon us."

"Is it not a bad idea to forget?" Father asked, not looking up from his work. "Even failures can lead to better things."

"What are you trying to tell me father?" Aiko asked. "Is there some kind of lesson that I am supposed to learn from this?"

"I do not know what lesson you should learn," Father replied. "You are making of me what you want to make of me."

"Well I suppose that our relationship never really did recover after all of this," Aiko commented. "It probably should have made it stronger, or made us closer but it didn't. After realizing all we lost I just kept staring at the mountain."

"In what way?" Father asked.

"Well this was traumatic," Aiko explained. "I was a pretty sheltered kid. You guys knew that I had issues socializing with others and making connections with people. I was gifted and you and mother let me pretty much focus on whatever I wanted. Then one day, almost literally the world around me opened up and swallowed most of what I held dear. I decided that I could not trust the world, I could not trust anyone. The only solace I found was looking forward and things that I could have effect over … machines."

"You made a choice?" Father asked. "To become one with machines?"

"I always liked to build, always liked to see how things went together," Aiko replied. "I originally thought that I wanted to build houses and buildings, perhaps be an architect. However, this event, the one I cannot seem to escape, taught me the futility of building things on places that were not as permanent as they appear. That is when I turned to machines, which could be put anywhere really and if they fall and get broken, I could always fix them."

"There is wisdom in that," Father replied. "But sometimes it is a good idea to know what things can be fixed and what things need to be left alone."

Aiko looked at her father.

"That is a really strange thing to hear from you. My father was a bit of a control freak and would be unlikely to hold such an ideal."

"Well we both know I am not your father," Father replied. "But I can offer ideas nonetheless."

"Then who are you then?" Aiko replied. "My subconscious? My fears? My unresolved family issues?"

"I am what you made of me here," Father replied. "I did not know what to expect or what I would find."

"Wait," Aiko replied, her brain struggling to process everything. "Who are you?"

An alarm beeped and it startled Aiko awake. It seemed that whenever she was trying to reconcile her dreams she was always interrupted. This was part of the job as astronauts could never expect a fill night's sleep. She looked over and saw that it was the com.

"Yeah?" She replied after hitting the burton, unwilling to really focus on much more pleasantry given the circumstance.

"This is Mack," Mack said over the comm, their voice seeming tired and frustrated. "We are having issues with the remote signals being jammed by the ground current. Do you have any solutions?"

Aiko rubbed her eyes, trying to reconcile how groggy she felt. "There's a relay transmitter in sector four. I can put it to a different frequency and it should no longer pic up any interference."

"Can you do it from there?" Mack asked. "We kinda need this up and running."

"No," Aiko replied with a sigh. "I got to go out and do it ... I will get geared up and go get it in twenty."

"All hands are out here," Mack replied. "You ok if I just send Sam to escort you?"

"That is fine with me," Aiko admitted, realizing she would actually enjoy seeing Sam. "Have him meet me at the northern airlock."

"Confirmed., Mack replied before signing off.

Aiko acted like she was on autopilot. She put on her spacesuit, suited up and got ready to go outside. She knew what she had to do for the transmitter, going over the relatively simple procedure in her mind. Her dream still nagged at her. What was her father in her recent dreams representing. It was like her mind was trying to tell her something and she could not quite make up what it was. Maybe it meant something, maybe it didn't, Aiko could not decide which.

"Lovely day for a stroll," Sam said as he rolled up with his tripod module as the door to the airlock finished its opening cycle.

"Are you trying to add levity to distract me from what is going on?" Aiko asked as she headed out onto the Martian landscape.

"You see right through me as always," Sam replied. "It is my job to try and keep the crew in check with their emotions. I come equipped with the ability to always be devoid of distraction so I try and pass it on to the crew."

"Makes sense to me," Aiko said as she walked toward her destination. She noticed that all the modules seemed to have been pulled into a perimeter as if they might be used to defend the camp in some way. "Though I do not know how much I could be helped I do appreciate the company."

"Sometimes just having a sounding board is all one needs," Sam agreed.

"I mean that you are my friend Sam," Aiko admitted. "I appreciate your company."

"Well I thank you Aiko," Sam replied. "I enjoy yours as well."

"Is that weird?" Aiko asked. "That I imprinted so much emotional attachment onto you?"

"Not at all," Sam replied. "It is shown that humans frequently attach emotion and even humanlike traits onto other things. They transpose complicated traits to animals, machines, and even intimate objects. A thing that has always fascinated me is human's obsession with naming intimate objects and drawing faces on things."

"I suppose some of us are just inherently lonely," Aiko replied. "We can feel alone in a room filled with people and sometimes objects we imbue with personality are much easier to relate to."

"Are you feeling alone right now?" Sam said as Aiko came up to the transmitter and began to take a panel off to work on it. He rolled around to be right next to her. "Are you feeling you cannot relate to the others?"

"The situation more than the people," Aiko admitted as she worked. "I want to relate to them but we are seeing parts of them that are making bad decisions and lost in a sea of uncertainty. I can imagine the others are feeling the same."

"They are indeed," Sam replied. "We are the first to be doing what we are doing and there is no real precedent for things that go wrong here."

"That is one way to put it," Aiko admitted as she finished her work and closed her panel. "Aiko to Mack … did that fix the problem?"

"Stand by," Mack replied before a several second pause. "There seems to be no interference now."

"Ok perfect," Mack replied. "By the way can you go over to sector five with Sam? There is some kind of resonance within the field and we just want to see if it is anything."

"Yeah," Aiko agreed. "Send me co-ordinates."

Mack sent the information and Aiko and Sam headed over. She still felt numb like nothing was real but as she came around the corner from a bunch of crates and stopped dead in her tracks. A small object stood before her as if it had been set up just for her.

"Sam … is that what I think it is?"

"It would appear so Aiko," Sam admitted. "That is the laser drill you left behind in the alien cavern.

***

Aiko set up the laser cutter on the tripod in her lab. She had reported that it was simply a piece of equipment that was causing the disturbance and she would take it in for analysis. Only she, Sam, and Prof knew the significance of the laser device and no one found it strange that she took it inside. She finished setting it up in the middle of a diagnostic area, Sam in a cradle nearby.

"Alright," Aiko said as she looked at the cradle. "I need to know for certain if this is in fact the one we left in the cavern."

"I am checking it now," Sam began. "Though we have two more in our stores this one matches the serial number and electronic designation as the one you used."

"Sam, is there any chance one of the others could have gone in to get it?" Aiko asked, her mind still in shock.

"I have gone over the turn of events and I believe that is not possible," Sam explained. "Someone would have had to go back past you to take it and somehow come back past you to bring it up, then hide it. Also, due to my estimation of the cave-in it would take either a heavy digging module or several days of excavation to retrieve it."

"So, it must be them," Aiko commented. "Doesn't it?"

"That would appear to be the most likely scenario," Sam responded. "What do you think this means?"

"I think it means they got the message," Aiko replied. "Otherwise this machine would hold no significance to them."

"It also means that they directly did something else," Sam replied. "They manually brought this machine back and left it within camp for us to find it."

"Pull up surveillance cams," Aiko commanded. "Tell me when and how this thing showed up in camp."

"Working on it," Sam replied as a nearby screen came on. It showed the area in the sector the device had been found. One minute there was nothing, then a spray of dirt as the device rose into place and stopped as the dust settled.

"How long before I found it did this occur?" Aiko replied.

"This occurred just one minute before Mack saw the disturbance on the sensors and called you," Sam replied. "It was not there long before you arrived.

"Was anyone else within the area?" Aiko asked. "Anyone else that might have found it if I didn't go to it?"

"No," Sam replied. "You were the closest to it by far."

"I know what I am about to say is crazy but does that not sound like they chose to leave it near to me?" Aiko asked. "Or could it just be a big co-incidence?"

"I am more inclined to assume in coincidence usually," Sam replied. "Though in this case the signs do point to deliverance."

"So, they wanted to show us that they got the message and that they know it was in fact me who sent it," Aiko commented. "I think they also know we lost someone down there. They returned what was still intact."

"I must admit if it were the remains of Coz returned it would most definitely not help the situation," Sam remarked. "They already think the aliens are killers."

"Well we need to talk to the aliens," Aiko replied. "We need to find the evidence to clean all of this up."

"That would be rather problematic," Sam replied. "All connections to the radio equipment is being currently monitored as per Havoc's orders. Even if you found a workaround it would require extensive subterfuge."

"Yeah with all the trust and issues that is less than ideal," Aiko agreed as she leaned back in her chair. "Also, we still might have a saboteur and it would be bad to tell them we are back in communication with the aliens."

"What do you intend to do?" Sam replied. "Ty and convince Havoc to give you unrestricted access to the radio systems?"

"I don't know," Aiko admitted. "He has a lot on his plate right now and is kinda stuck on protection mode. Even if I could convince him I was right he would still have to convince mission control."

"You believe that you are certain?" Sam asked. "Certain about the aliens and their intentions?"

"I am not at a hundred percent on it," Aiko replied. "I am almost certain they do not mean us harm but I still do not know what they want. If I try and pitch the case I will undoubtedly be asked if they don't mean to hurt us what do they want?"

"Undoubtedly so," Sam replied. "As that is the real question."

Aiko nodded.

"We need to find another way to contact them, one that requires far less sub-systems and something that cannot be traced by the saboteur."

"That is a tall order," Sam commented. "Even with your technological abilities that would be hard to guarantee."

"Yeah," Aiko agreed. "Also, the saboteur seems to have a skillset beyond what we know of the others. There's literally no way to gauge how close they are to my level of security that I would put in place. It would just be a guessing game and hope that it was secure."

"Well I believe in your ingenuity," Sam replied. "And as long as it does not interfere with the safety of the mission I will do what I can to support you."

"Thanks Sam I ..." Aiko replied.

Feeling suddenly lightheaded, she started struggling for breath, spots appearing in her vision. Aiko acted fast, getting up and walking over to one of her space suits that was in the bay. It was the one with the cracked visor and it was on her list to repair. She held her breath, struggling to keep what useable oxygen she had left and struggle to put the helmet on. It had some air trapped inside it and she took a small controlled breath. She felt the spots begin to fade but she knew she would not have much consciousness left.

"Aiko there appears to be a fault in the oxygen regulation system." Sam replied. "I am trying to access it but it will not respond."

Aiko hastily started putting on the rest of the suit. She knew that her breath would not last long and again the lack of oxygen would make her begin to feel dizzy again. She had been getting faster and faster with her suit and knew that this time it did not need to be perfect. She was not in a vacuum, just a low oxygen environment. She skipped all the steps she could skip, soon pressurizing the suit and falling to her knees as she gasped for breath.

"Aiko, are you alright?" Sam asked.

"I think so," Aiko replied as she slowly stood up and caught her breath. "I suppose I was just lucky to have had a suit in here. Is anyone else inside and hit by this."

"No, it seems just regulated to this compartment," Sam replied.

"Sam are the cameras in here running?" Aiko asked.

"No, they are not," Sam replied. "It appears that there is an interruption."

"I think someone is trying to kill me Sam," Aiko replied. "The air gets dropped in the compartment only I am in and the cameras are off so they can do whatever they want."

"It does seem that way," Sam admitted. "I think I can counter the controls and get the air back in here in a few moments."

"Wait," Aiko replied as she walked over to her table. "Whoever is doing this does not know they failed yet. Leave everything as is and instead let's see what else they are up to."

"You think the attempt on your life is only a distraction?" Sam asked.

"It might well be," Aiko said as she pulled things up on the tablet. "It looks like someone is trying to gain command control over the whole system."

"Shall I stop it?" Sam replied. "That would be very bad."

"No," Aiko replied. "Well yes, stop it. However, can you put in a dummy layer in the ships systems so it looks like they have control but when they go to use it the system locks them out, alerts us and tells them that they have to manually access the computer core to restore control?"

"An elaborate ruse," Sam agreed. "I will do it. As long as they don't immediately test it we should fool them … at least for a while."

"They wouldn't test it," Aiko agreed. "The moment they take control everyone will notice. They likely will wait until just the right time to strike."

"It is in place," Sam replied. "I cannot tell who is accessing our system but they now likely believe they have control of it. Also, it seems the air is coming back, the cycle they programmed seems to be done with its job."

"They are assuming I am either dead or unconscious," Aiko replied. "And you are too busy reacting to the issue to notice what they were really doing."

"It is true," Sam replied. "Had you not told me to search for a breach I would not have done one now."

Aiko nodded.

"This makes it really hard for me to believe I can talk to the aliens without worrying about sabotage."

"Indeed," Sam replied. "I worry as they could be trying to get back into contact with us as it is."

Aiko stopped, "You are right, they might have already." She got up and walked over to the laser cutter turning it on.

"You think there's something with the cutter?" Sam asked.

"Sam, can you connect to the cutter and tell me if it is still set to cut the symbol of our cells?" Aiko asked.

"Accessing," Sam replied. "No … there appears to be another image in its place. I cannot make any sense of it."

"Prime the laser to cut it into an object," Aiko said as she placed a small flat steel scrap on the floor by the drill. She then checked the oxygen level and began to take off her suit.

"The laser is priming," Sam replied. "Why are you removing your suit?"

"The saboteur does not know their plan failed," Aiko replied as she finished removing her suit and stowed it in a nearby box. "I am going to pretend to be unconscious to keep up the ruse that we did not know what they did. You will also need to pretend to be in diagnostic mode."

"Unconsciousness was a reasonable assumption as an outcome of this," Sam agreed. "I think this is a really clever plan."

Aiko nodded as she finished staging the area like she had indeed fell unconscious, placing things to look like they were knocked over like she fell from her seat. She looked over as the laser came to life, cutting a pattern into the steel scrap. Aiko went over and picked it up. It was a series of dots. She walked over and showed it to Sam.

"I can make little sense of it," Sam replied. "It is most definitely not a cell."

"It seems to be something else," Aiko replied as she slowly turned the scrap over, the dots seeming to make sense of an image. As she stared at it she realized that it approximated a set of mountains, a very specific set in Japan on Earth.

Aiko gasped, "Shit."

"What is it?" Sam asked. "What does it mean?"

Aiko looked to Sam.

"It means the aliens have been in contact with us for a lot longer than we think."

Chapter Six: Answers in the Sand

The attempt on Aiko's life was underplayed, much to Aiko's intentions. She figured that if she had really been hit by the attack and survived, she would not know what had happened during the event. She figured the less her would-be attacker knew about what she knew the better. The idea that it was a glitch was easy to portray as it was in fact Aiko who would oversee finding out if it was or not. The saboteur had left a trail of breadcrumbs to make it look like an accident and all Aiko had to do was pretend to believe it.

She went over in her head who the attacker and saboteur could be. There were not options that made sense. Every name that she offered to herself of the crew was met with overwhelming reasons why it could not be them. She decided that she would find out soon enough, she had set the trap in the main computer and it would soon become the time to confront them.

The eventual confrontation offered a different challenge. How would she do it? She considered telling Mack or Havoc, but given the circumstances, she did not know for sure that she could trust either of them. What if she let in to Mack, for example and they were in fact the saboteur? Aiko would be offering herself up on a silver platter. She had a lot to think about, a lot to play and not too much time to do it.

There was still much work to do, even with the stoppage of regular work there was a lot of upkeep to the station that had to be kept up with. It was easy to forget they were in a hostile alien environment and that there was a thin line between them and horrible deaths. Even with the apparent threat of alien invasion, they could not afford to let things go unchecked when it came to their survival.

After a day or two there were no events, attacks, or anything that escalated the situation. The base was still in defensive mode but people were starting to find time to do some of the myriad of experiments. Ivy worked on her greenhouse, Prof did tests, and Aiko had time to do as she wanted. First on her list was contacting the aliens.

There had been not a peep from them but there was still a thing hanging over her head. They knew about the mountains in Japan, a thing that she barely even talked about. This was a strange dilemma that seemed to make no sense. Aiko stared at the piece of metal, trying to disprove it being what it was. However, it was too clear, too specific. She did not have to look up the mountain in the databanks, it was seared into her mind in every detail and the markings matched it in every way.

This led to a harder problem to solve … how had the aliens known about the mountain? Even if they had somehow heard her talking about it, how could they recreate it? Aiko knew the outcome of the thought experiments but was not ready to reach it yet. Maybe they heard her talk of it and looked it up in their databanks somehow. That idea was impossible because they would have no way to recreate her exact viewpoint without seeing it. Aiko struggled for ideas but what it came down to was that they somehow saw her dreams. This is when Aiko noticed that there was a dead space near the bottom of the laser carved illustration. At first, she thought it was nothing but dead space but as she looked at it she came to a realization.

"The dead space is me!" Aiko said to herself. "This is not my perspective … it is my fathers!"

Aiko then struggled to remember all the strange things her father had said to her, all the unreconcilable things. Most were hazy but she recalled something about him being what she made of him.

"Sam, I need you," Aiko said into the comm. "We have a … situation."

Sam rolled into the room in one of his modules. "Are you alright Engineer Aiko?"

"I need to talk to you about the aliens," Aiko replied. "I think there is a development."

"Please go ahead," Sam replied. "I have been eagerly waiting for you to tell me about what was found on that laser carving."

"Sorry," Aiko replied. "I played that one a little too close to the chest."

"It is alright," Sam replied. "I am literally built to be patient."

"The aliens knew something," Aiko began. "They knew something that only someone in my dreams would know."

"Your dreams?" Sam asked. "I do not wish to be skeptical but I am having issues realizing how that is possible."

Aiko nodded, "I understand Sam. This is kinda a weird situation … however this whole thing, everything around is by definition unprecedented. Let us operate under the assumption that they did indeed look into my dreams. How would they do that?"

"Luckily for you I am one of few machines that can operate on what if scenarios," Sam began. "I would imagine that they are not indeed … psychic, and would need some manner of access."

A switch flipped in Aiko's brain, "Sam did you not say that there were things that you do to help us sleep?"

"Indeed," Sam replied. "But it is a simple thing. There are machines that use the comm system to emit low frequency waves imperceptible to the human ear that are meant to sooth humans under stress and help them reach deeper REM sleep."

"So basically, you are blasting radio waves into our brains?" Aiko asked. "And what are these aliens seemingly fond of using?"

Sam paused, his mechanical mind whirling and making noise. "Keep in mind this is all theoretical science and we do not know all of how the human brain works. But the idea is that these radio waves are interacting with the natural electro chemical functions of your brain. It would make sense that it would be like a radio transceiver of sorts."

"These dreams that I have been having are nothing new," Aiko explained. "But ever since we have reached the theoretical range of the aliens influence they have been more intense, like it is trying to get me to go through it. I thought it was for me to reconcile it all but what if it was the aliens trying to figure me out? The complexity of the dreams has grown as the aliens understanding of us grew. Maybe they did not know how to quantify what they were seeing originally and each time it made more sense."

"There seems to be a lot of evidence supporting this hypothesis," Sam admitted. "For example, this dream is something you described as troublesome and brings you back to a more troubled time in our life. You would be exuding stronger signals and ones that are very likely very specific."

Aiko nodded. "So, what if, during one of their first probing's of us, even before discovering the module they encountered my mind through the radio waves. They did not know what it was but it was strong enough to interact with. There were dozens of things connecting our ship to Mars that we did not even think to check. The module was a more direct line they could figure out but my mind was something more complicated and harder to use."

"It does make sense," Sam replied.

"Wait," Aiko said, more ideas flooding to the forefront of her mind. "What if I am not the only one that has been contacted in this manner?"

"You think that the others might have encountered the alien intelligence in their dreams?" Sam asked. "That is a reasonable hypothesis."

"Well for me it was an intense dream of loss and regret," Aiko began. "What if others are having similar bad dreams and do not know that the aliens are trying to communicate with them."

"Well, you took the dreams as a negative psychological state," Sam replied. "You, however, have been focusing on working through it and led the aliens to a greater understanding. It is reasonable to think the others, if so effected would just think it was a bad dream."

"Should we cut off the sleep radio signals?" Aiko replied. "Perhaps the saboteur is reacting negatively to the contact."

"Well, that is a mixed bag," Sam offered. "Assuming that the alien contact is happening to the others and someone is reacting negatively from it, the sudden cut off from it might further fuel their paranoia. If they are even aware of it, the sudden change might spur them to more drastic action."

"Yeah, that is true," Aiko replied. "I just wish there was a way to know. Perhaps I could ask the others if anyone is experiencing bad dreams?"

"I do not think there is a point," Sam admitted. "I would say that most likely, most of the crew is not aware of the dreams and might not even remember them. If anyone was indeed having negative dreams and suspects there is a problem, they would likely not tell you the truth and then they would know that there is someone else experiencing the same and it would make them a target."

Aiko sighed, as much as she wanted to figure out the situation she knew that most things she would try would only make things worse. She was frustrated that the only real developments about the aliens were negative and the only people who seemed to be able to do anything about it were the people who were protecting the group from them and the saboteur. This was the time for answers and Aiko could not afford to wait any longer. However, an idea came into Aiko's head, one so simple she could not believe that she had not just jumped to it originally.

"Sam … we are forgetting the biggest thing here."

"And what is that Aiko?" Sam asked.

"That they indeed are communicating with us in dreams," Aiko admitted. "We just need to find a way to guarantee they link up with us and make it a stronger signal."

"Interesting," Sam replied. "Well, it is possible that we could induce a deeper sleep state. Prof would very easily give you some sort of medication to do that. I also can amp up the signal. It might be uncomfortable but should give them more access and keep you in a much more vivid state."

"Then we need to do it," Aiko stated. "I will go under tonight and demand answers, and demand them now. This is literally threatening to go sideways at any time and we need to know what is going on. The saboteur has some sort of master plan and it is very likely against the aliens. I can't tell their motivation or why it started, but it seems that they want to take them out and do not care who gets hurt in the process."

"Normally it would be my job to say this is a risky idea and dangerous," Sam commented. "But I am at a dilemma on how best to protect this mission and the crew and this might be the best way to do it. I will help you in this any way that I can."

"It is our best shot," Aiko agreed. "Let's go."

As anticipated Prof was fine with the idea of giving Aiko a mild sedative. They had talked about her trouble sleeping before and he gave it to her with no questions asked. Aiko finished the rest of her tasks and later went to her sleeping area to set everything up. She rigged an amplifier next to her bed and Sam would be personally present to regulate it. Aiko took the sedative and laid down in bed. Her heart was racing and she tried to anticipate what was coming and what to say. However, as she began to grow drowsy the ideas began to fade away. She could not really prepare for what was about to happen. All she could do was hope for the best and that she would finally be given her answers.

***

Aiko stood in a small park, she could smell the grass and feel a breeze over her body. She looked around and saw a hospital behind her. It was a couple of days after the earthquake and her father was inside working on the seemingly unending amount of injured. Aiko waited in the park, trying very hard not to ask questions of what ifs about her mother and grandfather.

Aiko shook her head, remembering this was a long time ago and she was older, and not even on Earth anymore. She turned, looking for her father, finding him standing several feet behind her.

"I know who you are now," Aiko stated confidently. "You are not really my father."

"This was a face that you put on me," Father replied. "I did not much understand it but it has become somewhat clearer."

"I know that you are who I have been communicating with here," Aiko commented as she stepped forward. "You are a being that lives on Mars!"

"That is one way to put it," Father replied. "But you are not mistaken."

"Have you been in contact with us for a long time?" Aiko asked. "How did it start?"

"When we became aware of your vessel," Father replied. "As it left Earth and locked onto some manner of signal from something here you sent."

"The navigational beacon?" Aiko asked. "How is it possible you detected us on Earth."

"I must explain our history," Father replied. "For that to make sense."

"Please do," Aiko replied. "I would love to know that … is it the history of your people on Mars?"

"Partially," Father admitted. "We are originally from a world very far from here. We were plentiful but began to enter a phase in our evolution where we needed very little. Our planet was changing and grew difficult to survive so we decided to set out to see what other worlds we could colonize, much like yourself."

"Mars is a colony?" Aiko asked in shock.

"It is," Father replied. "We built vessels, two of them. This one we sent out to a world that we felt had the best range of survivability. We do not much care for heat, and the cold depths of this planet were perfect for us. The vessel was made up of not only our bodies but the building blocks to alter ourselves to the new environment. We are now part of this world, living within its sand and creating for ourselves only what we need."

"You aren't just in the sand you ARE the sand?" Aiko asked, trying to figure it all out.

"We are beings that are always in a state of flux," Father admitted. "It is like thought, everchanging and not often still. When we were able to connect to you, we thought you were like us … but as much as your thoughts were accessible, we struggled to understand the finite state of your physical forms."

"We have but one body each," Aiko admitted. "That must have been hard to reconcile?"

"It was," Father admitted. "As adaptable as we are, we found what we saw in your race much less so. It seemed that the ones we contacted were ridged, unable to see past single moments in a brief mortal existence. That is why we tried for a secondary, more direct line of communication."

"The module," Aiko replied. "That is why you used it to contact us."

"You must understand we do not perceive things like time and space as you do," Father continued. "We can traverse distance and portray thought in an instant. The idea of interacting on a direct plane is difficult for us. You seem to be focused on what is going on right in front of you and we had nothing to present to you at that time in that way. That is why we adopted signals and tried using analogies."

"Well, we are communicating very well right now?" Aiko commented.

"This is not a here and now kind of situation," Father admitted. "This is a world built of memories and impulses in your mind. This conversation takes but seconds … for you it seems to play out in your real time, but for us is nearly instantaneous … this is the best amalgam of our two ways of thinking. When we first came into your minds, we did not know any way to take stock of what we were experiencing. Some of your minds were too hard to read or rejected our influence outright. Only two of you seemed susceptible and you are proving to me the most amicable … the other mind is much more chaotic."

"There is one among us that is not reacting well," Aiko admitted. "They have been lashing out and sabotaging us. They are the one who destroyed the symbol you made."

"It is likely they are one and the same," Father admitted. "You live in this moment of tragedy and change, they live in a moment of anger and hate. We have tried to communicate with them more and more, but as much as you moved from this moment to add to our understanding of you, they have proved unwilling to do so at all. They just grow more hateful, more violent."

"Who is it?" Aiko said. "If you could identify them to me, it would help me greatly."

"It is not so easy," Father admitted. "Though we are conversing well now, it is because we are accessing your intelligence and knowledge. We are not so proficient at your language, but as we are in your mind you supply us with ways to quantify that we are saying and meaning. Though I look like your father and can see you, it does not mean that we have much of a basis to tell one human from another in the real world. We do not know the name of the other we have contacted nor could we describe them in simple terms."

"Could you try?" Aiko requested, she needed to know which member of the crew tried to kill her and any advantage would be beneficial.

"The individual seems trapped in a moment of rage and pain," Father explained. "They are a warrior of sorts and a moment early in development forced them to do things they did not want to do. They were hurt and hurt others and this seemed to have sharpened their reality. They are violent, they are angry, and we fear that we have brought it out and to the surface. We have considered cutting off the connection to them but still wish to fix the damage. You have proven that your minds can grow and adapt and we wish it for them as well."

"Humans minds are fragile," Aiko admitted. "Even we don't know all of how they work. I was very hesitant to come to terms with this point in my life you have seen. Though I was suggested to face it and ironically you have helped me greatly."

Father smiled, "I am glad it led to both a greater understanding between us as well as a better version of your mind."

"I must ask though," Aiko interjected. "Have we hurt you in any way. The saboteur has done some unfortunate things as well as the fact we did much digging."

"The digging has not much affected us," Father admitted. "Though you have moved sand around a lot and set thing on top of it, we are not finite and the sand is still there. We inhabit it all and none of it at the same time. I realize this concept is hard to understand but your mission has not hurt us. However, the heat, the fire injured part of us greatly. The moving and disturbance of the sand does not hurt us but the heat does. When we made the glass, we were careful not to get too close. Your laser did not get too close. However, one of our kind was in the sand beneath the glass, wanting to alter it or respond and he was removed from the connection with the rest of us."

"I am sorry," Aiko replied. "That was the work of one of us and it saddened us that it occurred. We too lost one of our people."

"We know," Father replied with a nod. "His form was found in one of our older creations. None of us were there but a large force of destructive heat summoned us. It was there we found your symbol, your message, and your lost companion."

"We … miss him," Aiko replied, thinking about Coz and trying to hold her emotions back.

"When we lost part of ourselves we also regretted," Father said, trying to mimic an apathetic expression. "We are however not as individualistic as humans. Our existence is the sum or our parts and though we regret losing part of us we do not long dwell on it."

Aiko nodded, "Well there is something desirable in that. With our friend, we feel his loss deeply and regret that his death happened for no real reason. The saboteur set that explosion and we feel that his life was wasted in a senseless act of violence."

"Well if it makes you feel better, it was not for nothing," Father admitted. "We studied his remains and it lead us to an even greater understanding of your people. We once were like you. We had need of more complicated structures. Those tunnels were once a place we used to build in before we surrendered so a simple more efficient form."

"You are a lifeform that is far beyond our conventional understanding," Aiko admitted. "I want very much for our peoples to learn from each other and I regret that our first meetings were tainted by the rash actions of one of us. I am working as hard as I can to find out which one of us this is and to stop them. I fear that they are planning something big and it is up to me to stop them."

"It is not very easy for us to help you," Father said in an apologetic tone. "But in your world, we are still struggling to figure out how to react. We are close but still need more time."

Aiko nodded in agreement, "I just hope I can get you that time."

"Know that while your people hold much opportunity for violence we do not do so quickly," Father replied. "We prefer to build then to destroy."

"Some of us are better," Aiko admitted. "That is what we strive for in humanity but often find ourselves falling short of."

"Well we are as curious of you as you are of us," Father admitted. "We did not know what to expect when we realized you were coming to us."

"Oh!" Aiko replied as she remembered back to the beginning of the conversation. "You mentioned how you knew. Is it because of the other vessel like yours? Was there an attempt to colonize Earth like you did on Mars?"

"Not exactly," Father explained. "We made two but that one was not finished and never reached its final destination. We can communicate with it but decided to use it more of a satellite of sorts. It was not until your Mars beacon that we reactivated it."

"Earth was not the ships destination?" Aiko asked, confused.

"Not the destination," Father replied. "It was the point of origin."

***

Aiko's head spun when she woke up. She struggled to compartmentalize what she had learned, her mind not knowing the difference from a discussion and a dream. The aliens were in contact with her, they knew what was going on and she had some answers. She struggled with the implications that Earth was the origin of the alien species. She decided that it was likely due to the fact that Earth had likely been in an age the aliens enjoyed the Earth's temperature, leaving in favor of colder and dryer places in space. There was so much that she wanted to ask of the aliens, so much that she desperately wanted to know.

"Was the experiment a success?" Sam asked, still in his portable module.

"Very much so," Aiko responded happily. "We finally have some answers, a lot of them in fact … it's going to take me a bit to process all of this."

"Understandably so," Sam replied. "But the next challenge is ahead … now that you know what is going on … how best do you use this information?"

"That Sam, is a very good question," Aiko admitted, only having scratched the surface in thinking what she might in fact do about the situation.

Her thoughts were interrupted as she was summoned by Havoc to come down to ops. She hastily dressed and headed over to his position.

Havoc was standing over several monitors at ops. He seemed pre-occupied and as if he had not much slept. As Aiko approached he slowly turned.

"Aiko," He said with a nod, seeming to be trying to stay casual. "How are you doing?"

"Good I suppose," Aiko replied awkwardly. "What is going on?"

"I have my doubts," Havoc replied. "We are preparing for war up here and it seems as though we have done so rather fast. I wonder if maybe we might be in the wrong here. What do you think?"

Aiko almost told him everything she knew but something nagged at her. She remembered the alien telling her about the other one, the violent one, and their warrior memories. She did not want to entertain the idea that it might be Havoc, but the uncertainty nagged at her mind.

"What if they are the saboteur and this is a trick to see if I am on to them?" Aiko thought, deciding to choose her words more carefully until the trap on the computer was sprung and she had a greater understanding of the situation. She took a deep breath, composing her thoughts. "I think that we are going to be remembered for how we handled this situation. It is very hard, now that we are dealing with it to see clearly."

"You know there are a lot of commanders that are remembered fondly by history and many who are not," Havoc admitted. "I found myself wondering how this one would be? What if there are people who wonder why I would do what I did in this time and place. Would I be remembered well or remembered poorly?"

Aiko could not decide if that was just a melancholy thought of stress or some kind of confession about the other violence. She decided that all things considered that he had done things pretty well. If he had wanted to do more against the aliens, he probably would have the opportunity to do more. She was not yet ready to trust him with everything but could offer him something.

"I think you did what could be asked of no one else. You adapted well and though we have had lost. We are not lost."

"Yeah," Havoc said with a nod. "You must pardon me, I am just an old military dog wondering if he howled at the wrong moon."

"So, what is it you wanted to speak to me about?" Aiko asked, deciding to get back on topic.

Havoc nodded, snapping out of his uncertainty. "There are some requests and all of them are outside. I realize you are still recovering from the accident with the air recyclers so I wanted to know if you are alright to go in a suit again yet?"

"I am fine I think," Aiko replied, adding a tone of uncertainty to add to the illusion she had actually been in trouble. "It was like taking a nap and all things considered it could have been worse. I am ready to go out and take care of some things."

"Good," Havoc sad as he forwarded something from his tablet onto hers. "Seems everyone needs you today … I forwarded the requests."

"I will get to them right away," Aiko replied with a nod.

First on the list of requests was Mack. The intrepid pilot was on a module on the outer area of the camp. Apparently one of the observer modules had been rigged to circle the camp and search for anything out of the ordinary and broadcast it back to ops. According to the request, it was lagging to the right and after several routes around the camp had to be manually moved back to course.

Aiko put on her suit and met Mack as they stood by the module. Even in the space suit, Aiko could tell that Mack was stressed.

"How are you doing?" Aiko asked as she walked over and took out her tablet. "Other than the malfunctioning module."

"I'm alright," Mack replied. "Just stressed, but that is to be expected with all things considered."

Like Havoc, Aiko could not easily see Mack as being the violent saboteur, though they had the military background it seemed the gentle casual solder would not be capable of the same violence. Aiko then realized that she knew very little about Mack. So as Aiko went to work on the module diagnosing the issue, she decided to ask some questions.

"So how did you get into the military Mack?" Aiko asked. "You don't talk about yourself much."

"I don't usually like to," Mack admitted. "The person you see here, the pilot, the soldier, the astronaut is how I want to be regarded. My past is behind me and does not matter for much."

"I know that feeling," Aiko admitted. "I had things in my past that really bit at me. I pushed them behind me for years but recently have come to terms with them and feel much better."

"With all due respect, I will have to pass on that idea," Mack replied. "My coming to terms with things in my past was the act of putting them behind me. There are things that are part of who I am that I exist rather happily not sharing or letting come out again. Some things cannot be reconciled, some things cannot be dug up without causing more damage."

"I understand," Aiko replied, realizing that she should not push them. "It appears there is an issue with the guidance system not correcting for the terrain. Easy fix. It should go on its route with no problem now."

"Thanks," Mack said with a smile. "I hope this will all be over soon so we can go back to being explorers again."

Aiko smiled, she wanted to feel reassured, she wanted to rule Mack out but there was still so much in the air. It seemed that everyone had some sort of opportunity to do the other events and it was hard to discount any of them. Normally such things could be broken down to simple detective work but on Mars there were too many variables. The saboteur proved to be a master of the modules and even if they weren't there for something, there is a very good chance they could have altered the modules to do it. Aiko finished up a last diagnostic of the module and left Mack to go back to work. Next up was Prof and the search for answers would continue.

Aiko caught up with Prof who was working on one of the repair modules. The work order said it kept refusing to switch to the next materials packet once one ran out and needed to be manually reset. These were the kind of glitches that were not uncommon and usually required an easy fix.

"Aiko so good to see you," Prof said in a relieved tone. "I like to think I am good with machines but this one is baffling me. I went through diagnostics but everything shows as green."

"Well, then it means it's something much simpler," Aiko admitted, pulling out a screwdriver and removing one of the panels. "Something the computer cannot recognize."

"I have been meaning to ask you," Prof began. "Have we had any more contact with the aliens?"

Aiko wanted very much to tell Prof what she had experienced but since she could not eliminate anyone she decided that she could indeed not trust anyone. "Nothing, I have been too busy to look really."

"I am not sure if I believe you," Prof replied, his voice growing more serious. "You were so closely connected to them, surely they have tried."

"If they have tried to directly contact me, it would have fallen on deaf ears," Aiko replied, telling a certain version of the truth. "We haven't exactly been very open to them with all that has gone on."

"Well I am worried," Prof admitted. "Just because we are not listening does not mean they are not saying anything. Who knows how long they will accept being ignored."

"Well, there is not really much that we can do Prof," Aiko admitted. "We need to focus on making sure everything is safe."

"We could plan something," Prof suggested. "Just you and me … like the laser thing."

"Prof that was hard even before things went terribly wrong," Aiko admitted, not wanting to mention Coz being the biggest issue about that catastrophic day. "There will be time soon to deal with everything but we got to focus on other more immediate things first."

"Well we can only hope that it is not too late," Prof replied. "And that we do not regret acting faster."

Aiko felt increasingly uncomfortable. Prof had always been kind of obsessed with the aliens and he seemed to be able to focus on little else. Luckily Aiko found the source of the issue and was able to change the subject.

"Here is the problem. There was a small fleck of debris over one of the levers that leads the next cartridge. With it where it was, it always assumed the cartridge was full. I removed it and it should work perfectly now."

Prof tested the machine and seemed to find it was indeed working well. "Thank you, Aiko. I'm sorry if I got too intense."

"It is alright," Aiko replied. "It is an intense planet."

Finally, Aiko went in search of Ivy. Her suit was beginning to feel heavier and her muscles sluggish. It was easy to forget you were wearing a space suit, but when you did it was always more than happy to eventually remind you. The work order said that a machine kept disconnecting from the remote on a cultivator. Being one of the diggers, this was concerning indeed. She came up to the module and found Ivy waiting for her.

"Sorry it took so long," Aiko said in an apologetic tone. "Been a bit of a long day."

"Oh no rush," Ivy replied. "If I have learned anything in botany, it is that things take time."

Aiko set up her tablet and immediately discovered a problem. "This one is easy. With all the increased use in monitoring the perimeter this module is having issues staying connected to the base. This is not the first time I have had to fix this issue. I can switch it to a different channel and it should be fine."

"I am so sorry to drag you out here for something so simple," Ivy replied, "I just, you know assumed the worst when it stopped working. I look at these things now and assume they are all on the verge of attack."

"It's quite alright," Aiko admitted. "I admit to always triple checking them all now. I just hope that things will get better around here."

Ivy nodded. "I suppose that is all we can hope for. I still will grow grass on this planet. I made that promise."

"Remember when you told that over the broadcast?" Aiko said with a laugh. "Seems so long ago."

"It does," Ivy said with a laugh. "Thigs have the way of turning out much different then you thought they would. I suppose it really is up to us to adapt."

"I agree," Aiko replied as she doublechecked the module. "Though you should be fine to continue now."

"Thank you, Aiko," Ivy replied happily. "Once I get back to work I will feel much better about things."

"Me too," Aiko replied with a sigh. "Me too indeed."

***

Aiko was soon back in her lab, barely rested from the spacewalk when she got an urgent message over the comm.

"Aiko, they are attempting to access the main computer," Sam explained.

Aiko went to a monitor and pulled it up and looked at what was going on. "They are attempting to knock out the full comm system."

"What do you want me to do?" Sam asked.

"Make it look like they have succeeded," Aiko replied. "Keep our comms open, but let them take the rest down."

"Affirmative," Sam responded. "It also seems like they are disengaging the safeties on module engine fault detection."

"What would that accomplish?" Aiko asked. "What would trigger it if it was left on?"

"A myriad of things," Sam replied. "It mostly regulates the internal engines of the modules that have generator drives."

"Generator drives?" Aiko asked. "You mean the ones with batteries that can threaten dangerous consequences if compromised?"

"Yes," Sam replied. "Any one of them could cause a very potent explosion."

"Sam, I want you to stop that change from happening, but make it look like it did," Aiko demanded as she ran over and began to get into her space suit. "Also, see if you can back trace any information on what they are doing or if any of the modules have been linked in this way."

"Working on it," Sam replied. "I set up the block and reroute, but I am detecting a large buildup of energy coming from a module in Sector 4."

"Which one?" Aiko asked, still getting dressed. "And can you stop it?"

"I cannot tell," Sam admitted. "They have gone to great lengths to cover their tracks. I can tell you the exact location of the disturbance."

"Link it to me," Aiko replied. "I am going to stop it manually."

"Should I call anyone?" Sam replied. "It will take me time to reroute the communications but I can …"

"No!" Aiko interrupted. "You might just be telling the saboteur we are coming. Get a module, something you might be able to defend me with and meet me there."

"I am on the other side of the compound," Sam replied. "It will take some time."

"Hurry," Aiko replied, checking her suit. "If I can't shut this thing down, we are in for some serious trouble. I need to go now!"

"Be safe," Sam replied. "I will join you soon enough."

Aiko left the airlock. She knew that she was supposed to tell Havoc about it, but admitted with the comm being mostly down she could not if she wanted to. Assuming he was not the saboteur she could only imagine the chaos that he was experiencing in ops. The first matter of business was to get to the site of the overcharging reactor and shut it down, everything else was secondary. She realized that it had to be one of the modules she worked on today. When she was doing open diagnostics with her own tablet, it left them in an open state. If the saboteur wanted a way in to gain access to the reactor controls, they would probably find that time a good time to do it. Aiko cursed herself for not thinking of that but it moved her mind to figure more out. If it was someone with her when she accessed it that would mean that that Prof, who did his own diagnostics and caused Aiko to skip her own could not be it. That left Ivy and Mack, neither of which was someone Aiko wanted to be the saboteur. The idea then occurred to her that it was indeed Havoc that had sent her out so urgently to accomplish what looked like minor issues. He linked to her tablet before she left and it could have been him. It seemed the more she tried to figure things out, the more elusive the answers became.

"Aiko, we have a bit of a situation," Sam cut in. "I am still a few minutes away from rejoining you, but I need to let you know."

"There is an explosive about to go off on Mars," Aiko replied, fighting the fatigue in her body. "I fear to ask how it could possibly get worse."

"Well it can," Sam replied. "I was cross-referencing the geological surveys and saw that there is a material in the soil about thirty meters down. This module seems to be at least partially buried so that means it is closer."

"You got to cut to the chase Sam," Aiko demanded. "I am running on fumes when it comes to energy here, and I need to focus on not passing out."

"The material is highly conductive," Sam explained. "The saboteur probably thought by burying it that it would not cause the base to be damaged beyond repair … however in my initial simulations of the material and surrounding geology I am confident that if it goes off, this area will be reduced to a crater the size of a small city."

"Yeah that is much worse," Aiko replied, feeling her fear and concern tighten, adding adrenaline and making her move faster. "Seems to have put a bit of a second wind in me. Thanks for setting that fire behind me Sam."

"No problem," Sam replied. "I just hope you can put it out before it's too late."

Aiko moved as fast as she could and when she got to the sector found a large hole. It was more than large enough to hold the module which seemed to be mostly covered up in sand below. Aiko did not have time to identify it or figure out how the hole was dug, instead taking out her tablet and trying to connect to the module locally now that she was close enough.

"Aiko!" Havoc called out, bounding around the corner in his suit. His suit automatically connecting over the still functional local comm. "What is going on?"

Aiko looked at him, noticing that he was carrying one of the space guns, one hand on it. "Why are you here? How did you get here so fast?"

"I detected the energy build up," Havoc replied. "The comms are down so I came as fast as I could to investigate."

Aiko looked at him suspiciously, the idea that he had linked to her tablet in ops came back into her mind. "You are the saboteur?"

"No!" Havoc assured. "I am trying to smoke them out as much as you. Please give me the tablet, let me figure out what is going on?"

Havoc began to move forward, standing on the edge of the crater and reaching out his hand. "Please … let me see what's going on … I can fix everything."

"No!" Aiko said, stepping back. "You want to blow this place up because you think it will kill the aliens. They are much wiser then you think and that will only cause all of us to die."

"You are confused," Havoc replied. "But I assure you things are very different then you suspect."

Aiko stepped back again and Havoc suddenly went ridged. A hole had appeared from nowhere in his suit. Alarms flashed as he looked down, blood coming out of the wound and flowing out into the near vacuum of Mars. Havoc lost his balance, falling into the hole beyond. Aiko turned, seeing a lone figure standing a few feet off, a space gun in their hand.

"Y-you!" Aiko said as she turned to the newcomer. "You are the saboteur …"

"I am," Ivy's voice said over the comm as she slowly walked forward, aiming the space gun at Aiko. "I was not sure whether you were on to me or not. Figured the near-death experience might have thrown you off the scent."

"It was you, all of it," Aiko replied. "You destroyed the alien symbol, rigged the module to attack, you destroyed the cavern that killed Coz, all of it!"

"Very true," Ivy said as she reached to a pad on her arms, typing into it as she kept her gun pointed at Aiko. "NASA hired me not just for my botany skills. I am an ex PARA special ops soldier. I am known for getting the job done at all costs. Things like sabotage, demolitions, and breaking into weapons lockers are kinds like my special skillset. Mission control knew that there might be some things that needed to be done off board for this mission and they sent me the code to do it."

"But they do not know what is all going on here!" Aiko pleaded. "They think the aliens are hostile because you skewed it as such. All of the hostility, all of the violence … it is because of you."

"They have invaded my mind!" Ivy shouted. "They keep showing me things, horrible things from my past. They want to destroy us!"

"They don't, I assure you!" Aiko explained. "They have been accessing our minds through the radio signals that help us sleep. They did this to understand us and mean us no harm. They found a moment in my dreams that I feared and used it to figure me out. They have only seen negativity and violence in you."

"You are trying to trick me!" Ivy replied, punching things in to her pad. She then repointed the gun at Aiko. "Why can I not access the module anymore?"

"My tablet has admin access," Aiko admitted. "It locks the rest out."

"Turn it off!" Ivy demanded.

"Ivy listen to me," Aiko pleaded. "The site here is above a conductive mineral. You think you can blow it and destroy this sector but if you set it off the whole region goes under ... yourself included."

"These bastards are going to kill us anyway!" Ivy shouted. "They have a thing in orbit, and there's one on Earth! We need to stop them!"

"I can't let you do that," Aiko replied, lifting up her tablet. "I can't let you hurt them and destroy us just because you are confused."

"Don't move!" Ivy said as she stepped forward, the rifle still aimed at Aiko. "The only reason I have not shot you already is that we might need you after this. You touch anything on that pad and I will shoot. I want you to toss it to me."

"No," Aiko replied, looking down and realizing if she left the module in diagnostic mode, clicking one field, it would automatically power the machine down. "I can't let you make this mistake."

Aiko reached down and went to hit the button ... on the surface of Mars there was no way for her to hear the gun go off, even if she knew the sound it made. However, the bright flash was something she could see. She hit the button, commanding the module to stand down and the flash lit up her visor then suddenly stopped. Aiko instinctively closed her eyes, expecting to feel massive pain and the beginning of a suit decompression. However, neither happened and when she opened her eyes she was presented with a bizarre sight. Before her was a humanoid figure of sand and rock, formed in the seconds before the shot. It had taken the blast, hardening and crystalizing in order to block it.

Ivy was shaking, looking around as two other forms flowed up out of the sand and began to move toward her. They were like humanoid in shape but mostly featureless. Their faces were familiar, mimicking a specific human face.

"Coz?" Aiko asked in shock, staring at the one that had saved her.

"No!" Ivy shouted, shooting the space gun at alien after alien. They did not seem to be damaged, some falling apart just to reform again. She staggered back, trying to regroup. "You will not destroy me!"

"You need to stand down Ivy, it's over," Aiko commanded. "They will not let you set off another bomb here. They won't let you kill anyone else."

"I have a mission," Ivy said, shooting another alien and dodging around another. She used the lower gravity to bound forward, reaching the edge of the pit. "I shoot that battery, it still goes off."

"Ivy don't!" Aiko shouted, stepping toward Ivy.

However, Ivy stopped cold, a hole appearing in the helmet of the suit. She slumped backward, falling lifelessly to the sand at the edge of the crater, the gun landing next to her. Aiko moved over to look in the pit, seeing Sam in one of his modules crouching over Havoc who still had his space gun aimed up at where Ivy stood.

"Sorry for the delay," Sam replied. "I got here just as he fell and had to move fast to save him."

"I could have been killed Sam!" Aiko replied, her heart still racing. "You could have at least told me you were here!"

"It would have likely only provoked her," Sam replied. "Besides I had no real recourse in that situation then to save Havok ... he did have the other space gun."

"Can we discuss this later," Havoc replied in a pained voice. "I still have a god dammed space gun hole through my shoulder."

"Sam get the comm back on and have Prof prepare the med bay," Aiko ordered.

"One step ahead of you," Sam replied. "He is readying it now."

***

Six months later things had become finally become quite peaceful in the Mars basecamp. The aftermath of Ivy's near destruction of the camp lead to a lot of work and a lot of questions. Mission control indeed did give her orders to do what needed to be done to protect the mission, but she had been feeding them misleading information about the aliens and their intentions. To mission control, it seemed as though one of their hidden assets was giving them the real story and it was about hostile aliens and a mission on the precipice of invasion. Now that she had been dealt with and mission control learned the full scope of her lies, they apologized and left all decisions to the site to Havoc and Aiko.

The aliens, though able to mimic human form still could not easily communicate. Sam and Aiko rigged up a radio array and immediate messages could be shared back and forth. However, Aiko proved best able to communicate with them and did so frequently. The aliens helped bring the fallen module back to the surface and even helped stabilize the site. They offered to assist in various activities on the surface and seemed very keen to help. Aiko pitched the idea that the aliens be considered part of the mission and their help was to be accepted.

Aiko and the others all watched a view screen as a craft streaked through the sky, it was the next crew and the continuation of the mission. They made an approach then came around for a simple landing, similar to that had been done already. NASA did not know if this second crew would turn out to be a rescue crew, be turned around, or if the mission could carry on.

Aiko and the remaining crew went out, with Sam driving a payload module behind them. As the relief ship opened its doors several aliens formed out of sand and stood in poses with arms out in peace … something Aiko had taught them. As the crew disembarked it seemed that their own AI computer was on a module and filming it, likely for NASA back home … very likely not live, the world at large was not ready for aliens … at least not yet. A tall astronaut in a space suit walked up, saluting to Havoc and the others.

"Captain Rodger Tutman, reporting for duty," The man said proudly. "But you can call me Pathfinder."

"Well met my friend," Havoc replied. "Took you long enough to get here."

"Heard you got shot with a prototype laser rifle," Pathfinder replied with a laugh.

"We call them space guns," Havoc replied. "Hurts less than a bullet, but still not something I would recommend."

The broadcast was wrapped up and the new crew was brought back inside. It was a celebration of sorts, welcoming the new faces and discussing what was to be done next. Aiko was reminded of a time when her crew was in such bliss, unaware of the hardships to come.

A few days later the core of the craft was being prepared for departure. Mack was to fly it back and any who did not want to stay and be part of the mission could return back to Earth. Aiko wanted to stay, which was a relief to NASA as she was the official emissary to the aliens. Havoc was also staying, a shot to the shoulder with a space gun did not much lessen his enthusiasm for the mission and the things they could accomplish. NASA eagerly offered for him to remain in command and he accepted it. Prof had decided to leave, his faith in the mission seeming to have been shaken.

Havoc and Aiko waited with them next to the door to the return ship to say their goodbyes.

"Won't be the same without you my friend," Havoc said as she shook hands with Mack. "I have to train the newbies from scratch."

"They will be better for it," Mack replied. "I am a pilot not an explorer. My place is at the controls. Who knows, I might come back in a couple of missions. If you are still here, we might see each other sooner than you think."

"I think this is not just the mission I was assigned to but a mission I believe in," Havoc replied. "I wish you the best and will await your return."

"Never noticed how beautiful this world was," Prof said as he took one last look. "Part of me will miss it."

"Well no one here will forget you," Aiko said, her voice uncertain. "We will miss you."

"As we will miss you as well," Prof replied. "I will be in charge of helping NASA figure out how to reveal this to the world. They know as well as any they can't keep this a secret forever and it would be better to tell the world on their own terms then to let a hacker or cyber-attack leak it."

"Well, I know you will share your wonder in them with the world," Aiko said with a smile. "Soon we will be united, our people and theirs."

Soon the return vessel climbed out of Martian gravity, to begin its long journey home. Aiko and Havoc went back inside … there was so much work to be done.

Epilogue

Aiko stood at the edge of the dock, the one that rested on the lake near her grandparents' house. Now that she had come to terms with the dreams, accepted their meaning and circumstance she found it to be a quiet place of solitude. This was where she went to meet with the aliens and this was why she was here now.

"You show much happiness here now," a familiar voice replied.

Aiko turned, seeing the alien she usually conversed with in a different form, that of Coz.

"You look like Coz," Aiko replied.

"Is this not alright?" Coz replied. "We figured due to his unfortunate loss and the fact we modelled our bipedal forms on him, this would be more accurate an avatar to converse with you in."

"It is fine," Aiko replied. "I think he would have enjoyed living on in this way."

"Good," Coz replied. "We have much to discuss."

"Indeed," Aiko asked. "There are members of the new crew that would like to be contacted through dreams."

"It would be our pleasure," Coz replied. "Turn on the devices and we will contact them. I presume they have been told what to expect?"

"Of course," Aiko replied. "They will have a much better time reconciling it now that they know what is coming."

Coz nodded, "I am glad that this ended the way it did … losses aside, it is fulfilling for us to have continued contact with your people."

Aiko nodded, "I agree. However, I wanted to ask, why did you abandon Earth?"

Coz looked out over the lake. "It is similar to this lake and the land around them. An unfortunate event changed things. The Earth was very dry for a long time, then very cold. We flourished deep within the earth but soon the climate began to change. In the short term, we knew that we would have to adapt to survive and in the long term the Earth would end up very different. We saw other forms of life, those made of carbon beginning to develop. We figured we had the means to move our civilization so we would do that, allowing what would form on Earth to form. When the vessel in orbit of Earth proved unnecessary and flawed we decided to leave it … in case some time … many millions of years later, life arose on Earth and warranted contact."

"I cannot imagine being from such an ancient species," Aiko commented. "Humans only have a few thousand years of recorded history and evidence of not much longer. Compared to you we are but children."

"Time becomes quite relative in evolution," Coz admitted. "That was why it was so hard for us to relate to you at first. We had to stop regarding time by eons to think of the here and now. It will still take much time to get used to it but it is necessary. Someday, I have no doubt, humanity will evolve to being more like us in that regard and it is worth waiting for."

"Well, that depends on what we do here," Aiko replied. "On Mars, I mean. Humanity is definitely not ready for aliens on Earth, but on Mars, they can see you, get used to you, and learn the benefits of our co-existence."

"There are so many benefits," Coz agreed. "Though we are more advanced than you in so many ways we, like you, have not much experience with life forms different then our own. We have many questions and have only begun to understand your culture and your science."

"Well, I am just glad that we have connected," Aiko replied with a sigh. "Humanity is young as I mentioned. We tend to treat new things we do not understand with suspicion and violence. Ivy almost destroyed everything."

"Do you see her as a villain?" Coz asked.

"Actually, I do not," Aiko admitted. "She was a friend and as much as we can condemn, we can also forgive. In the case of the history of this time, I think she will be remembered most of as an example. She displayed the distrust, paranoia and the violence humanity is capable of. You saw it and are still willing to see the best in us."

"We saw you at your worst and your best," Coz replied. "As a species, even a young one, your best is worth it and leads to amazing potential. This potential is what we are most looking forward to seeing you reach to … in the individuals we know and as a species."

"I agree," Aiko replied with a nod. "I have done a lot in my life so far but the thing that I look most forward to accomplishing is seeing where this goes for our people. We are at the dawn of a new age … both of us and it's anyone's guess where it goes now."

No more words were shared as Aiko and the alien stared out of the gentle waters of a lake frozen in time. There would be a lot to do in the coming weeks and years, but Aiko enjoyed the small moment outside of time as a way to reconcile everything that had happened … and what would happen next.

THE END, or is it THE BEGINNING?